dialect of a skirt
erica miriam fabri

Hanging
Loose
Press

HOLD TIGHT:
THE TRUCK
DARLING
POEMS

JENI
OLIN

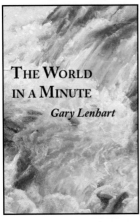

THE WORLD
IN A MINUTE
Gary Lenhart

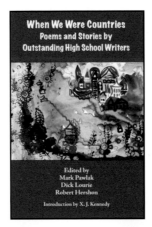

When We Were Countries
Poems and Stories by
Outstanding High School Writers

Edited by
Mark Pawlak
Dick Lourie
Robert Hershon

Introduction by X. J. Kennedy

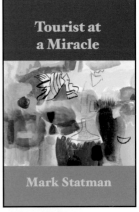

Tourist at
a Miracle

Mark Statman

3/03

a novel by
chuck wachtel

VACATIONS ON THE BLACK STAR LINE
MICHAEL CIRELLI

2010–2011

SELECTED BACKLIST

BOOKS BY SHERMAN ALEXIE

THE BUSINESS OF FANCYDANCING: THE SCREENPLAY. 157 pages • Paper, ISBN 978-1-931236-27-7, $16.00 • Hardcover, ISBN 978-1-931236-28-7, $24.00. Signed & numbered hardcover, $100.00.

ONE STICK SONG. Poetry and Prose • 96 pages • Paper, ISBN 978-1-882413-76-8, $15.00 • Hardcover, ISBN 978-1-882413-77-5, $25.00 • Signed & numbered hardcover, $100.00.

THE SUMMER OF BLACK WIDOWS. Poetry • 139 pages • Paper, ISBN 978-1-882413-34-8, $15.00 • Hardcover, ISBN 978-1-882413-35-5, $27.00.

FIRST INDIAN ON THE MOON. Poetry and Prose • 116 pages • Paper, ISBN 978-1-882413-02-7, $14.00 • Hardcover, ISBN 978-1-882413-03-4, $27.00.

THE BUSINESS OF FANCYDANCING. Poetry and Prose • 84 pages • Paper, ISBN 978-0-914610-00-7, $15.00 • Hardcover, ISBN 978-0-914610-24-3, $27.00.

....

Eula Biss, **THE BALLOONISTS.** Prose • 72 pages • Paper ISBN 978-1-931236-07-2, $17.00. Hardcover ISBN 978-1-931236-08-9, $27.00

Ha Jin, **WRECKAGE.** Poetry • 111 pages • Paper, ISBN 978-1-882413-97-3, $14.00 • Hardcover, ISBN 978-1-882413-98-0, $22.00 • Signed & numbered hardcover, $100.

Robert Hershon, **CALLS FROM THE OUTSIDE WORLD.** Poetry • 77 pages • Paper ISBN 978-1-931236-57-7, $15.00. Hardcover ISBN 978-1-931236-58-4, $25.00

Hettie Jones, **DOING 70.** Poetry • 92 pages • Paperback ISBN 978-1-931236-72-0, $15.00. Hardcover ISBN 978-1-931236-73-7, $25.00

Joan Larkin, **MY BODY: NEW AND SELECTED POEMS.** Poetry • 149 pages • Paperback ISBN 978-1-931236-74-4, $16.00. Hardcover ISBN 978-1-931236-75-1, $26.00

Mark Pawlak, **OFFICIAL VERSIONS.** Poetry • 111 pages • Paper ISBN 978-1-931236-59-1, $15.00. Hardcover ISBN 978-1-931236-60-7, $25.00

Mark Pawlak, Dick Lourie, Robert Hershon & Ron Schreiber, Eds, **SHOOTING THE RAT: OUTSTANDING POEMS AND STORIES BY HIGH SCHOOL WRITERS.** Poetry and Fiction • 280 pages • Paper, ISBN 978-1-931236-23-2, $16.00 • Hardcover, ISBN 978-1-931236-24-9, $26.00.

Steven Schrader, **WHAT WE DESERVED: STORIES FROM A NEW YORK LIFE.** Fiction • 198 pages • Paper ISBN 978-1-931236-63-8, $16.00. Hardcover ISBN 978-1-931236-62-1, $26.00

M. L. Smoker, **ANOTHER ATTEMPT AT RESCUE.** Poetry • 64 pages • Paper, ISBN 978-1-931236-51-5, $14.00 • Hardcover, ISBN 978-1-931236-52-2, $24.00.

Keith Taylor, **GUILTY AT THE RAPTURE.** Poetry and Prose • 78 pages • Paper ISBN 978-1-931236-61-4, $15.00. Hardcover ISBN 978-1-931236-64-5, $25.00

Terence Winch, **BOY DRINKERS.** Poetry • 76 pages • Paperback ISBN: 978-1-931236-80-5, $15.00. Hardcover ISBN: 978-1-931236-81-2, $25.00

Bill Zavatsky, **WHERE X MARKS THE SPOT.** Poetry • 109 pages • Paper ISBN 978-1-931236-67-6, $15.00. Hardcover ISBN 978-1-931236-68-3, $25.00

Keep in Mind...2009 Titles

Sherman Alexie, **FACE**

"This is Sherman Alexie's first collection of poems and short prose since 2000, the same kind of mix that caused *The New York Times* to say of his first book, *The Business of Fancydancing,* "Mr. Alexie's is one of the major lyric voices of our time." *Face* is the winner of the Paterson Poetry Prize and is number one on Small Press Distribution's 10-year best-seller list.

Poetry • 160 pages • Paperback ISBN 978-1-931236-70-6, $18. Hardcover ISBN 978-1-931236-71-3, $28.

Jack Anderson, **GETTING LOST IN A CITY LIKE THIS**

"His latest collection reveals all his wit, his wayward charm, and the innocence that allows him his shocking honesty...."—Edward Field

Poetry • 98 pages • Paperback ISBN 978-1-931236-97-3 $18. Hardcover ISBN 978-1-931236-98-0, $28.

Jayne Cortez, **ON THE IMPERIAL HIGHWAY: NEW AND SELECTED POEMS**

"Cortez has been and continues to be an explorer, probing the valleys and chasms of human existence. No ravine is too perilous, no abyss too threatening for Jayne Cortez."—Maya Angelou

Poetry • 131 pages • Paperback ISBN 978-1-931236-90-4, $18. Hardcover ISBN 978-1-931236-99-7, $28.

Dick Lourie, **IF THE DELTA WAS THE SEA**

If the Delta Was the Sea fuses Lourie's work as a poet and a musician. "*If the Delta Was the Sea* is a genuine delight."—Ha Jin "Presented with irony, humor and honest insight."—Martin Espada

Poetry • 132 pages • Paperback ISBN 978-1-934909-01-0, $18. Hardcover ISBN 978-1-934909-02-7, $28.

Charles North, **COMPLETE LINEUPS**

Charles North's ingenious poems in the form of baseball lineups have been exhilarating readers since they first appeared in 1972 and sportswriter Larry Merchant devoted two *New York Post* columns to them. Includes drawings by Paula North.

Poetry and Art • 69 pages • Paper ISBN 978-1-934909-03-4, $18.

Elizabeth Swados, **THE ONE AND ONLY HUMAN GALAXY**

A "strange and beautiful book.... A must read."—Harvey Shapiro. "A triumphant debut."—Honor Moore

Poetry • 133 pages • Paperback ISBN: 978-1-934909-07-2, $18. Hardcover ISBN: 978-1-934909-08-9, $28.

Hannah Zeavin, **CIRCA**

"This extraordinary first collection by Hannah Zeavin is circa another century when the old weird America and the world at large strummed its imagination with a searing song."—Anne Waldman

Poetry • 55 pages • Paper ISBN 978-1-934909-09-6, $16.

VACATIONS ON THE BLACK STAR LINE
Michael Cirelli

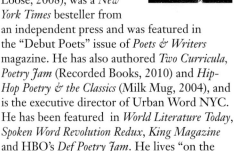

Michael Cirelli's first collection, *Lobster with Ol' Dirty Bastard* (Hanging Loose, 2008), was a *New York Times* besteller from an independent press and was featured in the "Debut Poets" issue of *Poets & Writers* magazine. He has also authored *Two Curricula, Poetry Jam* (Recorded Books, 2010) and *Hip-Hop Poetry & the Classics* (Milk Mug, 2004), and is the executive director of Urban Word NYC. He has been featured in *World Literature Today, Spoken Word Revolution Redux, King Magazine* and HBO's *Def Poetry Jam*. He lives "on the moon."

Poetry • 96 pages • Paperback ISBN 978-1-934909-20-1. $18.

THE WORLD IN A MINUTE
Gary Lenhart

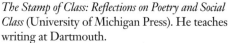

This is Gary Lenhart's fourth collection of poetry. He has also published two other recent books, *Another Look: Selected Prose* (Subpress) and *The Stamp of Class: Reflections on Poetry and Social Class* (University of Michigan Press). He teaches writing at Dartmouth.

"Gary Lenhart's *The World in a Minute* combines all the best of intellect and heart. This compendium of histories takes in the political, ranging from ancient Rome to the Vietnam war to the present; the personal, which verges on memoir in its reminiscences of his life from its working-class childhood roots; and an intimate look at his relationships in the world of art and literature."— Cleopatra Mathis

Poetry • 58 pages • Paperback ISBN 978-1-934909-12-6 $18.

DIALECT OF A SKIRT
Erica Miriam Fabri

Erica Miriam Fabri's work has appeared in such publications as *The Texas Review, Hanging Loose, The Spoon River Poetry Review, The New York Quarterly* and *Good Foot Magazine*. She is also a spoken word mentor and curriculum writer for Urban Word NYC. She currently teaches creative writing and performance poetry at The School of Visual Arts, Pace University and for the City University of New York (CUNY) at Hunter College and Baruch College. This is her first book.

"These aren't poems. They're ball gowns."— Rachel McKibbens

"In Erica's impressive first collection we hear a myriad of characters speak—some hilarious, some ironic, some tragic—and we can't help but listen. And learn." —Sharon Mesmer

Poetry • 88 pages • Paperback ISBN 978-1-934909-10-2, $18.

Find out about author readings and reviews on:
hangingloose.blogspot.com

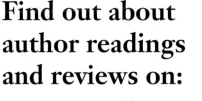

HOLD TIGHT: THE TRUCK DARLING POEMS
Jeni Olin

A native of Houston and a resident of New York, Jeni Olin studied at Oxford and Cambridge before receiving her BA and MFA degrees from Naropa University. Her work has appeared in *The Portable Boog Reader, The Hat, LIT, Hanging Loose,* and many other magazines.

This is Jeni Olin's second full collection of poems, following her exciting debut, *Blue Collar Holiday.*

Writing about that book, John Ashbery praised her "wonderfully caustic and vulnerable lyrics," adding that "Olin's voice is both raw and strangely accommodating. This is a marvelous debut."

Poetry • 106 pages • Paperback ISBN 978-1-934909-14-0, $18.

3/03
Chuck Wachtel

Chuck Wachtel is also the author of the novels *Joe The Engineer,* winner of the Pen/Hemingway Citation; *The Gates;* a collection of stories and novellas; *Because We Are Here* (all Viking-Penguin); and five collections of poems and short prose, including *The Coriolis Effect* and, most recently, *What Happens to Me,* both published by Hanging Loose Press. He lives in New York and teaches in the Creative Writing Program at N.Y.U.

Praise for Chuck Wachtel's fiction: "Wachtel achieves a gripping narrative because his eye for nuance and detail is exceptionally vivid, and because his knowledge of his characters' lives, the emotions they bear, is direct and unsparing." —*Minneapolis Tribune*

Prose • 159 pages • Paperback ISBN: 978-1-934909-07-2, $18.

TOURIST AT A MIRACLE
Mark Statman

Tourist at a Miracle is Mark Statman's first full collection of poetry. His poems, translations, and criticism have appeared in many anthologies and in such publications as *American Poetry Review, The Hat, Hanging Loose, Tin House,* and *Florida Review.* Statman is an associate professor of Literary Studies at Eugene Lang College of The New School and also taught for many years for Teachers & Writers Collaborative.

"It's very rare to watch the birth of a new style. It's like watching through a new set of Proust's kaleidoscopes. Mark Statman has been working for years on a vision of himself and parts of the city—concentrated and bare as any poetry."—David Shapiro

Poetry • 88 pages • Paper ISBN 978-1-934909-16-4, $18.

WHEN WE WERE COUNTRIES: POEMS AND STOIES BY OUTSTANDING HIGH SCHOOL WRITERS
Edited by Mark Pawlak, Dick Lourie and Robert Hershon

When We Were Countries is the fourth volume in this highly praised series.

Praise for *Shooting the Rat*: "Images leap from the pages full of surprises, from classical allusions to brand name references, presenting readers with sharp slices of life and a variety of philosophical musings. The prose pieces – some stories, other captured moments – showcase writers who have mastered their craft and found their voices." — *VOYA (Voice of Youth Advocates)*

Poetry • 280 pages • Paper ISBN 978-1-934909-05-8, $19. Hardcover ISBN 978-1934909-06-5, $29.

Exciting New Books...

Hanging Loose Press
231 Wyckoff Street
Brooklyn, N.Y. 11217-2208

ADDRESS SERVICE REQUESTED

3/03

Also by Chuck Wachtel

What Happens to Me
Because We Are Here
The Gates
Sin Embargo (chapbook)
The Coriolis Effect
Joe The Engineer
The News (chapbook)

3/03

A Novel
and Commonplace Book

By Chuck Wachtel

Hanging Loose Press
Brooklyn, New York

Published by Hanging Loose Press, 231 Wyckoff Street, Brooklyn, New York 11217. All Rights Reserved. No part of this book may be reproduced without the publisher's written permission, except for brief quotations in reviews.

www.hangingloosepress.com

Printed in the United States of America
10 9 8 7 6 5 4 3 2 1

Hanging Loose Press thanks the Literature Program of New York State Council on the Arts for a grant in support of the publication of this book.

Art Direction: Robin Tewes
Cover design by Bill Kontzias and Robin Tewes
With photographs by Susanne Michelus and Bill Kontzias

Acknowledgments
Portions of this book have appeared in:

Signale Aus Der Bleecker Street, a bilingual anthology of contemporary writing from New York, Editor: Bernd Huppauf. Wallstein Verlag, Gottingen, Germany, 2005

WBAI, Pacifica Radio, 1/19/05
Throughout the day (the eve of George W. Bush's second inauguration) a tape of a brief excerpt, read by the author, was included in each segment of national news.

Hanging Loose #86

Witness, Volume XX , *Exile in America*, International Institute of Modern Letters, University of Nevada, Las Vegas, 2006

Library of Congress Cataloging-in-Publication Data available on request.

ISBN: 978-1-934909-18-8

 Produced at The Print Center, Inc. 225 Varick St., New York, NY 10014, a non-profit facility for literary and arts-related publications. (212) 206-8465

For Hettie and Joan,
all four of them

Contents

. . . *I no longer have a country: I no longer have a body. The shelling continues to shatter the songs of praise and the dialogue of death, stirring in the blood like light consuming insane questions.*

What am I searching for? . . . I want to find a language that transforms language itself into steel for the spirit—a language to use against these sparkling silver insects, these jets. I want to sing. I want a language . . . that asks me to bear witness and that I can ask to bear witness, to what power there is in us to overcome this cosmic isolation.

—Mahmoud Darwish

No matter how artful the photographer, no matter how carefully posed his subject, the beholder feels an irresistible urge to search such a picture for the tiny spark of contingency, of the here and now, with which reality has (so to speak) seared the subject. . . .

—Walter Benjamin

We can't leave the television. Every tank, every helicopter . . . Is that my son . . . ?

—Voice of an unidentified woman,
*Operation Iraqi Freedom, NBC
News Documentary, 2003*

Someone Who Could Be, Though Is Probably Not, an Exterminator

March 15–21

Everything written in these notebooks of mine has the characteristic of never claiming to be definitive. I note patterns of thought which form of their own accord, and I stop at the point of writing that they have no meaning, or that I'm about to say the opposite.
　　　　　　　　　　　　　　—Paul Valéry, *The Notebooks*

The war "could last six days, six weeks. I doubt six months."
　　　　　　　—Secretary of Defense Donald Rumsfeld, 2/7/03

1

His three-year-old daughter, sitting atop his shoulders, reaches toward the dense shaft of light suspended between the wide lens of an arc lamp, set up on the open back of a truck, and the windshield of a taxi, hitched to the back of the same truck, in which a scene will soon be filmed. They're standing in a small crowd packed into the space of sidewalk between the curb and the front of a fish store. Since the scene won't be shot until the truck and taxi are rolling, the onlookers have not been prevented from getting close.

The actor in the driver's seat, wearing an unusually large purple turban, and the woman playing his passenger, sit perfectly still, their heads turned away from the crowd and the glaring light. The Korean woman who owns the fish store is standing in front of them, close enough to the taxi to open its door. She's been playing a game with his daughter, periodically reaching up and touching her hand without turning around.

The light shaft, its edges as sharp as lines drawn with a ruler, is much brighter than the span of chilly sunlit air it passes through: he imagines that if his daughter could touch it she would not only feel its heat, but its dense substance, like hard-packed sand.

No one is talking.

❖

A thin buzz he hadn't realized he was hearing stops when the light goes off, and the bodies of the people pressed closest to his unbend and tilt back on themselves like tall grass after a prolonged gust of wind. The two actors turn forward and watch the hand gestures of the director, a woman in headphones with attached bead microphone, standing on the back of the truck.

"Tom," his daughter says—she has recently begun calling him by his first name in moments she urgently wants his attention—and begins to bounce and rock, which means she's ready to get down.

As he lifts her over his head the actor in the driver's seat turns toward them, suddenly—in his peripheral vision he must have seen something large falling toward him from above—and when he sees this man bending at the knees, setting his daughter on the sidewalk, he again turns away from the crowd.

Tom asks the woman who owns the fish store if she knows what they're filming, but before she can answer someone behind them says, "She don't know."

They turn toward the source of the voice. A tall woman exhaling cigarette smoke chopped into syllables, speaking so loudly that the people around them can also hear, says, "What they told us is that it's for television. I was here earlier, even before they got into the car." She points to the woman in the back seat. "I think that's Brooke Shields."

Tom and the fish store owner turn back to the taxi, both trying to identify some aspect of Brooke Shields in the near side of the shadowed face in the back seat.

"She don't know anything," the woman behind him now says, at lower volume, aiming her smoke-laden voice just at him since he had initially asked the question. "That's not why she's here."

Most eyes are on the director holding her arm raised with fingers extended and pressed together. When she snaps it forward the actress in the back seat suddenly becomes animated, speaking with dramatic emphasis, bouncing as she speaks, leaning toward the driver to make a point, falling back against the seat, then leaning forward again. Everyone close enough can now see that it might well be Brooke Shields, but no one outside the cab, except the director, in headphones, can hear, so people watch *her* as she listens thoughtfully—her repeated nods and the small changes in her facial expression—and try to construct a sense of what is being said.

It's the turban, even more clownishly oversized than the ten-gallon hat worn by Hoss Cartwright in *Bonanza*, that classifies what is being enacted as comedy. The woman who could be Brooke Shields is talking with frantic passion about something urgently important to her. The humor requires that it be something personal and familiar, and seemingly of little consequence—perhaps to do with her love life, or friends, or job—and the turban is meant to emphasize the fact that the actor wearing it, silently pretending to drive, doesn't understand a word she's saying.

✿

Tom is someone who constantly writes things in a pocket notebook, usually his thoughts and experiences and, when writing about himself, usually does so in third person. He also writes poems and stories, many of which grow from the words that collect in his notebooks, and has had the good fortune, for a number of years now, to see them published in books, though the source of most of his income is the university where he teaches.

The following Tuesday, early morning, he is sitting on the stoop of an apartment building on St. Marks Place, writing about having been on First Avenue with his daughter, watching them set up and rehearse the scene about to be shot. As he gets to the moment when the woman who could be Brooke Shields talks to the actor in the driver's seat, the front door of the building opens and a woman walks down the steps. Though there is room for her to pass, he slides over to give her more, and as she steps past him he smells the shampoo from her wet hair. He wonders how she regards him: this stranger so near the private place where she has just slept, woken, prepared herself for the day. When she reaches the middle of the sidewalk she turns, takes a single step down the block, then stops, turns back toward him and, with a look on her face that implies she is probably wrong, says, "You're not the exterminator, are you?"

He's not sure it's a real question. He smiles.

But she remains there, wanting an answer, so he shakes his head.

✿

He begins to write again, but has lost the trajectory that carries him from sentence to sentence, so he reads over what he just wrote in the hope of regaining his momentum, but what he's thinking now is that the language he's using has changed, even in the three days since he stood in the crowd with his daughter on his shoulders. The substance of words held inside for a week, sometimes even for an hour, can begin to lose mass, but this is something else—it's not just in the words, it's in the small silences between them, as well. In the days that have passed since the day he's now writing about, the darkening swarm of words shouted from headlines and newscasts, in speeches and press statements, has grown louder and louder, and within these words resides the insistence that the monstrous will of those who govern us is our will, too. That certainty has shouldered its way deeper into our vocabulary like a horse-mounted police officer wading into a crowd.

Now someone else walks down the steps of the building, a young man who, as if to think or remember something, stops, upon reaching the sidewalk, just where the woman had stopped a moment earlier.

"I'm not the exterminator," he says to the young man, imagining he will find this funny. If he, too, is waiting for one to arrive, it would almost be as if Tom had read his mind.

Instead, the young man looks at him, or toward him, but does not speak.

Suddenly embarrassed, Tom says, "The last person to come out of the building was looking for an exterminator—maybe five minutes ago, maybe less," and this time the young man doesn't even appear to listen. Instead, he walks back up the steps and through the front door and then, a moment later, walks out again holding a cell phone which he pokes numbers into as he walks up the block.

❖

After the last sentence in the notebook, Tom now writes, *The language he had expected to be using when he next found the time to write in his notebook is not the language he's using now. It has been altered, perhaps to an extent commensurate with the widened gap between his instinctive sense of who the people around him are, and who the headlines tell him they should be.*

The real question, he adds, *is why he had to say something at all when there was maybe a ten percent chance the guy would've known what he was talking about, and less of a chance, even if he did, that he'd find it funny?*

He then answers the question: *If someone else finds funny something he thinks is funny, he'll enjoy its funniness to a far greater extent than if he'd kept it to himself, which is another way of saying that by telling this guy he wasn't the exterminator he was acting on the against-the-odds hope that for a moment he could loosen the restraints that harness him to his own despair by making it a thing apart from himself.*

A faint trace of wet-hair-shampoo smell finds Tom's nose and he looks west, up the block where the woman, and just after her the young man, had walked and since passed out of sight. He then looks down at his notebook and writes, *We are all trying to keep at a distance the fact that we are on the brink of war.*

❖

Tom remembers now that the woman standing behind him in the crowd, the woman who told them she thought it was Brooke Shields in the back seat, had never stopped talking, and he knew that after he and the fish store owner had turned back to watch them rehearse the scene, his daughter—this entirely separate person, holding his hand—had continued to face her, and that what held her attention was not what the woman was saying, but the small clouds of exhaled smoke that shot from her mouth along with the words.

After they finished rehearsing the scene the fish store owner squeezed through the crowd and went back to her store. His daughter stepped right up to the taxi.

15

"They don't know anything," the woman behind him said, even louder, but his daughter was now watching the actor in the purple turban, who had begun making silly faces at her.

"They don't know anything because they're not *here* to know anything. They're just here for the money, only there's none left. They already melted the pot."

❖

After walking a block toward home, Tom and his daughter had stopped in front of a newsstand so he could scan the papers stacked out front. The bold certainty of the daily tabloid headlines felt like the weight of a bully holding him down by sitting on his chest.

"Tom," his daughter said, tugging his hand, nodding in the direction from which they'd just come. "Look." And when he turned his head he saw the blinding circle of light, pouring from the arc lamp as it was being eclipsed by a bus moving slowly behind the truck hauling the taxi up First Avenue.

Suddenly he felt her hand slip from his and before he could stop her she had crossed the distance to the greengrocer next door, where she grabbed a handful of purple grapes from a quart basket out front, and brought them to her mouth.

"No, Hettie," he told her, "those aren't ours," but she took another bunch, and squeezed them until the juice was dripping from her fist.

He took her other hand again, reached for his wallet, and started up the plywood ramp between the raised tiers of displayed fruits and vegetables toward the entrance of the store but stopped when he saw the owner, standing behind the cash register, just inside the window, laughing and waving him back.

"She's still in the Garden of Eden," the owner shouted to him, and then, laughing even harder, he pointed at Tom's daughter, who was still holding his hand, while trying to cram the entire mashed and dripping bunch into her mouth.

16

Tom reaches out from under the roof of the bus shelter to feel if the steady thin drizzle he'd walked through on his way here is still falling. No umbrellas are open and few cars have their wipers on but he sees a translucent curtain, as sheer as mosquito netting, suspended somewhere between his eyes and the lighted storefronts across Avenue A.

The invisible droplets collect into a chilly glaze on his fingers and knuckles and back of his hand.

It's the first day of spring. On the walk that brought him here he passed a woman carrying four Key Food shopping bags, two in each hand, crammed with large bags of potato chips, smiling broadly to herself, and then, soon after, two men, one tall, thin, pot-bellied, wearing a white T-shirt under an unzipped black leather jacket, the other short, wiry, ponytailed, younger, carrying a pair of drumsticks, one in each hand, walking in quick side-steps so he could face the other man as he spoke to him. The two were in this formation when he first saw them, and they maintained it through the fluid moment their three bodies occupied the same square of sidewalk. "Can you imagine . . . ?" the smaller one said as they got near enough for him to hear. "Can you imagine giving somebody the electric chair and *forgetting* to strap him down?"

He steps into the street outside the curbside entrance of the shelter, looks north and sees the bus, the size of a shoe box, swinging slowly into the downtown traffic from Fourteenth Street. The drizzle is getting stronger again. He thinks of the woman with her potato chips, the blue eye and arched eyebrow of the Wise Potato Chip owl peeking above the top of one of her white plastic bags, and the button on the front of her blue quilted down coat, with the word *WAR*, in red, inside a black circle with a bold diagonal line over it.

When he steps back into the bus shelter he can hear the light patter of raindrops falling onto the hard plastic roof. He takes out his notebook and a pen and writes: *He hopes that nothing—not the rain, not another person, not a thought that arises without being summoned—will disrupt the current carrying the story she is telling herself from its source somewhere inside her to her smiling face. Not before she reaches her destination, climbs the steps, sets down her bags, and opens the door.*

He steps into the street again, and sees the bus leaving the stop before the stop before his, nosing into the traffic approaching him. It's two-thirty. He's going to pick up Hettie at nursery school and has to arrive before three.

The moment he steps back inside the shelter an angry child's voice, its source close behind him, says, "Yeah?" He turns to see a young woman leaning against the back wall of the shelter, gazing down at the pointed toe of her shoe as it rubs the valley of sock-covered skin below the anklebone of her other foot. With his head turned, he smells his own skin, mixed with the smells of wet sidewalk and the damp wool collar of his coat.

"I thought you said 'diving,'" she says. "Not *driving*. . . . What? Wait. No, hold on a minute." She pulls a cell phone from a small holster clipped to the waist of her low-slung jeans and lifts it to eye level—only then does he see the thin wire rising to her ear— and looks at the small, luminous-green display monitor. "Shit. Not *her. No* way. No fucking way," her voice growing much louder than needed to overcome the scatter-legged tap dance the rain is now doing on the roof. "No way am I talking to *her*." She slips the phone back into the holster and says, "Yeah? It's my aunt. No, that's my Aunt Maureen. This is the other one, the wicked bimbo of the west. I'll call her back next year." After that she continues to listen, without speaking, for a considerable length of time.

A single passenger boards the bus at the stop before his. Though he can only see in brief, diminishing glimpses, each time the wiper blades sweep the rain from the windshield, he assumes it is someone old, because of the slow rate at which the bear-shaped silhouette pulls itself up the two steps, and because the driver waits, as the new passenger finds a MetroCard, then takes a step, turns, and lowers

18

him or herself into a seat at the front before pulling out—something a bus driver would never do for someone younger.

This small part of the near future he can predict: sometime in the next minute or two he will see, up close, this person now seated at the front of the bus.

"What?" the woman behind him says. "No." She slumps backwards and begins to rap her knuckle against the Plexiglas wall, much of which is covered with orange fliers announcing a peace rally that he and his wife and Hettie had attended two days ago in Union Square. Because the young woman so frequently says *What?* and because she says it so loudly, he thinks it quite likely that the person she is talking to is also using a cell phone and is also out of doors.

He begins to imagine a young man, walking down a street elsewhere in Manhattan, holding a cell phone against his cheek, telling the woman now standing behind Tom about this crazy guy who was sitting on the steps of his building when he left the other day on his way to work. *The guy just looked at me and said, "I'm not the exterminator." Do you believe it? This city's filled with crazos. What do you think he meant?*

Tom grew up in this city and since childhood he has always liked watching an approaching bus when it angles toward the curb in such a way that, for a moment, he can't see either side, only the front, which looks like a face—this one thing hasn't changed through the various designs of busses over the years—a wide, middle-aged man's face that is friendly, serious, and unchanging.

"Maybe," the young woman says, as the doors swing open—she remains in the back of the shelter: she's not getting on—"Or maybe not. The doctor said I could've had it for a long time. Remember, like eight years ago, in Maryland . . . ? *Hel-lo*. More like *twenty* stitches? The last thing I remembered was turning on the headlights and shifting into *Drive*, making sure the little red needle was pointing at the *D*. The next thing I know this three hundred pound EMT lady is pulling on clear plastic gloves and smiling down at me. The doctor said *that's* the kind of head injury that can cause it and you might not even know until years later."

It's a man, the passenger sitting behind the driver, and old, as Tom had assumed he would be. All he can see of him are his eyes, peering over the top of the opened newspaper he holds like a shield, squinting for focus behind the lenses of his thick-framed glasses, as if he knew that this younger man, the only person getting on, would be boarding the bus with the specific intention of observing him closely. Tom smiles toward him as he dips his MetroCard into the slot, and when the man raises his newspaper he immediately sees that two other riders on the half-full bus are holding open the same paper, *The New York Post*, displaying the same headline: "Steel Wave Rolls Toward Baghdad."

Two days ago, though it now seems much longer, a speaker addressing the crowd at the peace rally quoted the city council resolution opposing a preemptive, unilateral war against Iraq: "The city where 2,792 people were killed on 9/11, of all cities, must uphold the sanctity and preciousness of human life." People cheered wildly; people cheered with crazy, thunderous, tragic enthusiasm, still trying, against all evidence to the contrary, to imagine there remained some hope of preventing war. "A hundred and fifty other U.S. cities have also passed resolutions opposing this war," the next speaker, an actress, said. "The United Nations will not endorse it. The Pope opposes it." And then, shouting into the microphone, she ignited a chant: "The world says no to war! The world says no to war! The world says no to war!"

What none of the demonstrators knew was that the hours of that evening—as they stood in a park in Manhattan, holding placards and candles and children, listening to speakers and shouting and clapping and chanting—corresponded with the predawn hours in Iraq, and that Tomahawk cruise missiles had begun to strike targets in Baghdad. The fact that the war had already started would be revealed to them later, at home, in incremental doses of information presented by the TV news.

First, studio newscasters aided by off-screen voices are already reporting that shortly after air-raid sirens were heard in Baghdad, missiles began striking buildings in several parts of the city. They add that they have received no official word, but they quote the ultimatum issued by the president two days earlier: "Saddam Hussein and his sons must leave Iraq within forty-eight hours. Their refusal to do so will result in military conflict commenced at a time of our choosing." (Few of those now watching, however, had distilled this one sound from the general clatter of saber rattling: Saddam's remaining in Iraq did not seem sufficient reason to fire the shot that would begin a war; and besides, the when-you-least-expect-it theatricality of the phrase "a time of our choosing," made the threat bluff-like, semi-real, at most something that would occur further into the future.)

Ten endless minutes later an announcement from the White House press secretary makes its first appearance in a left-to-right word by word procession along the crawl between network logos and the day's closing Dow Jones average: *THE OPENING STAGE OF THE DISARMING OF THE IRAQI REGIME HAS BEGUN. . . .*

The first images: sudden mountains of light and smoke, fireworks-like scatterings of luminous cinders flowering within a dense shadow-scape of buildings, rise in silence behind the voices of reporters now using the phrases "targets of opportunity" and "decapitation attack."

Finally, just before ten pm, the president appears, and though he is already in place—hands clasped, forearms resting on the Oval Office desk—it is an arrival, because everyone, on screen and off, has been awaiting him. He speaks to them for nearly ten minutes, stiffly inhabiting the familiar and outdated persona of a leader addressing a home-front populace whose support he is assured of. Before signing off by blessing their country and all who defend her, he tells them, "Now that the conflict has come, the only way to limit its duration is to apply decisive force. And I assure you, this will not be a campaign of half measures, and we will accept no outcome but victory."

Learning this way, in small stages, with gaps of time between, can make each small portion of information almost comprehensible: a fragmentary history of the last hour isolated from all the hours before it and, as such, less monstrous than the whole into which these fragments could otherwise be assembled. Thus, these demonstrators, watching the news in their homes, would have had revealed to them the circumstances of the war their country had just begun, though the human fact within those circumstances had been entirely hidden from view.

This morning, as his wife and daughter slept, he rose and turned on the TV, already tuned to the cable news network they'd been watching for the last three days. A handsome anchorman, on the left half of the divided screen, was asking questions of a reporter standing in front of a column of tanks and armored vehicles moving slowly through a world made of pale sand and blinding, Gatorade-yellow sunlight. The anchorman was thanking and congratulating the reporter, embedded with the Seventh Armored Battalion, for his fine work in covering their operations. Also in conversation with the reporter in the field, whose split-second-delayed responses sometimes faded to scratchy static, was a woman newscaster who remained off camera. During the course of the report she reminded viewers that the reporter they were talking to was the one who, just yesterday, in describing the armored column passing behind him, had coined the phrase "steel wave," which, in a single day, had been uttered so often by newscasters and at press briefings, and had infiltrated our language so quickly, that it was already hard to imagine you wouldn't find it in a dictionary. And as the woman reporter spoke, the image of the handsome anchorman was replaced by a full-screen image of the reporter in the field, who, though technically in conversation with the off-camera anchorman and newscaster, addressed the Iraqi viewers he said he knew were watching as well. He asked them to look at the steel wave passing behind him and to reconsider any plans they might have of resisting the American forces. He then said, repeating yet again the phrase he had given our language, "This unstoppable steel wave will keep rolling until it has liberated Kuwait." The woman newscaster cut in quickly, intercepting whatever he might say next, and spoke a single, clearly-enunciated sentence in which she used the word Iraq four times.

Tom sat in front of the TV, through all the other war news and domestic news and the weather report, and through all the commercials for cars, investment services and personal computers, until the story looped around again. He wanted to make sure the embedded reporter had truly said *Kuwait*. He wanted to make sure the man had actually stood there, in the middle of this shit storm, in the middle of the frame of his TV screen, referring to *this* war as the war that had been fought against this same country more than ten years ago.

When the footage did return, the entire sentence had been deleted, as had the woman newscaster's attempt to steer him and the viewers back on course. But this time what he saw instead was how excited the embedded reporter was, how that excitement had made him lose track not only of his words and of the time and place they referred to, but of his fundamental reason for being there, to report the news on the ground: Standing in the eye of this historical moment, this single person, this fool, had looked straight into the lens of a camera and threatened a nation.

※

When he was a younger man, and the life he lived was very different from the life he lives now, Tom had used heroin, and as the bus drifts downtown in the current of midday traffic, he remembers one of its effects: it can cause you to hear a diminished version of your own voice, from inside, as you speak. That's why junkies often speak louder than necessary. It was the voice of the woman, practically shouting into her cell phone in the bus shelter, and not seeming aware of it, that reminded him of this.

The rain has again diminished to a thin drizzle, and as the bus crosses the wide intersection at Houston Street, he thinks back on what she was saying as he boarded the bus, about the accident she had experienced and the unnamed condition she suffers from, and another of heroin's effects on the human voice comes to his mind: a music that can coat the words with a shrill, childlike certainty that reassures the speaker of the truth of what he or she is saying, and, at the same time, preempts any disagreement on the part of the listener. Because it is such a transparent and vulnerable kind of authority, junkies serve to remind us that when we're talking to other people, we're usually talking to ourselves, as well. In this case, what the young woman's certainty, heroin-induced or not, attempts to make inarguable is that she is swimming without effort against the painful and dangerous current of her own fate and, therefore, possesses the ability to keep fear at a distance.

The young man he imagined on the other side of her conversation disappeared the moment she said that last thing, about the head injury, but now, opening his notebook, Tom summons him back into existence and continues his conversation with the young woman still inside the bus shelter.

※

"There's more to it than that," the young man says, sadly, into his cell phone.

"I want to hear everything," she says, just before a syllable-long beat of silence tells him she is getting another call. Then, "Shit. My aunt's

24

calling again. Why would she call me twice in like ten minutes? She's a real bitch but it could be important. Maybe I better take it this time. I'll call you later, okay? And remember: I want to hear every-thing."

As the bus slowly moves south, Tom stops writing but continues to dream the story:

The young man, walking down a street quite near to the bus stop where the woman he was speaking to is still standing—though he doesn't know that—is relieved that their conversation has ended. He doesn't want to lie to her, yet he certainly doesn't want to tell her the truth. The only reason he told her about the man who told him he wasn't the exterminator was so he could reveal a small part of what is weighing so painfully on his mind and, thus, if only to a small extent, lighten the burden. The lie, then, was not in what he said, but in all the things he had not said, and would not say later when she called him back: that he had spent the night with Helen, who is married to Eddy, the brother of the young woman who is now speaking to her aunt. His name is Sylvester, this man who spent the night with Helen, but is known to his friends as Syl. Syl has known Eddy and Helen since their college days, and he has always been hopelessly in love with Helen who, even a decade earlier, preferred Eddy. Still, Syl would do anything to win her love—even a moment of it. When they were seniors Syl, who was a computer engineering major, had hacked his way into the school's computers and changed her grades so that she could graduate cum laude. A year later he called a bomb scare into the midtown offices of the insurance company where she worked, and still works, because she'd told him she needed the afternoon off.

In all that time he'd never told Helen of his love for her. Then, one night last year, Eddy called from Thailand to tell her that business would keep him there a week longer than planned. They had tickets for a David Byrne concert, which Eddy had entirely forgotten about, so she went with Syl, who cancelled plans with the woman he was dating at the time to accompany her. Helen had wanted to be an artist back in college but after graduation, after marrying Eddy and starting her full-time job at the insurance company, she seemed to forget her ambitions—until that night, after the concert, when she confessed to him that she had started painting again, since Eddy was spending more and more time traveling

25

for business. If it is business, she added.

She showed him two new canvasses she'd painted since he left for Thailand. Then she asked Syl if he would do her a big favor.

"Anything," he said.

"Anything?"

"That's what I said," he answered.

She asked him if he would pleasure her with his tongue.

"That's a favor for me," he said, smiling, tears forming in his eyes.

"One more thing," she said. "While it's happening I want to sing that David Byrne song we heard tonight. You know, that old one he used to sing with the Talking Heads."

"Which song was that?" he asked.

"You know, the one where he goes, 'I'm painting . . . da da da . . . I'm painting again.'"

The dynamic they'd unwittingly established years ago in college, the effect of his undeclared love, had now made itself known to them both; and the mutual acknowledgment that it was the only substance holding them together caused it to manifest itself in more direct and escalating forms. Now, each time Eddy was out of town on business, Syl would visit Helen's bed. The things she'd ask of him got harder and harder to comply with. "You're a comatose patient," she said, early on in their transformed relationship, "who can't feel a thing I do to you." She'd tell him about a pair of shoes or a necklace she'd seen in a store window, and wanted but that she couldn't afford, and then added, "But I won't accept it as a gift if you buy it for me. Only if you steal it." In a restaurant one evening, she suddenly stood up, told him she had to pee, and left for the rest room bringing her half-filled wine glass with her. When she came back she set the now-full glass on the white tablecloth in front of him. "Cheers," she said.

Finally, one morning, not long ago, she asked him to pretend he was an exterminator. The night before, while they were having intercourse, she saw a roach scurry across the ceiling, and that morning, as she was strolling about naked, showering, putting on make-up, and then dressing, he was to walk around her apartment, pretending to kill mice and insects, and at the same time, he was to gaze at her longingly, but not so she could see, then leave without touching her. When he refused to

26

do it she became furious. "I'll find somebody else to be an exterminator,"
she said, and stormed out the door. She knew he'd be watching her from
the bedroom window, which looked out onto the street, so after walking
past a stranger sitting on the stoop, she stopped, turned toward him,
and asked, loudly, if he was the exterminator.

❈

Tom climbs the stairs to his daughter's classroom, breathing the same air that permeated the halls and stairways of the public schools he attended as a child: dust, steam heat, rotting fruit, a century of coats of oil-based paint that give off a smell which is somehow cognate with how the walls and floors absorb the voices of the children, then mix them together before echoing them back. He peeks into the classroom.

He is ten minutes early, and the children are sitting in a circle around their teacher, who is reading to them from a book with an orange dinosaur on the cover. He knows it's a book they also have at home, but he's not near enough to read the title or hear the teacher's voice, so he can't tell if it's the one about the human parents whose son is a brontosaurus, or the one about the dinosaurs having a wild dance party that lasts until they grow so tired, at the dawn of the Cenozoic Age, that they all fall asleep.

Usually, when he arrives early, he chats with the other parents waiting to pick up children, but none have yet arrived, so he sits on a child-sized bench just outside the classroom's doorway, takes out his notebook and writes, as he often does, a number of phrases from Anton Chekhov's notebooks:

When he laughs he shows his teeth and gums.

She is surly and smells of a vapor bath.

Two young officers in stays.

27

A schoolboy with mustaches, in order to show off, limps with one leg.

Whatever happens, he says: It's the priests.

He selects these five from the dozens of entries he carries in memory. Each is a thumbnail sketch, a moment reduced to the simplest particle of itself. He is certain that each of these small handfuls of words began expanding into a story the size of a universe as Chekhov wrote them down, and continued to do so, long after he closed his notebook and slipped it into his coat pocket. He doesn't copy them in an attempt to envision the people Chekhov observed more than a century ago, but to hitch a ride on Chekhov's desire to prolong the sensation of encountering them, not just for use in a story, but to add the moment to the accumulation of circumstances he knew to be his life.

Following this he writes:

An old man, peering over the top of a newspaper, watches a stranger get onto the bus.

A man asks, Could you imagine giving someone the electric chair and forgetting to strap him down?

A woman carrying several bags of potato chips, smiling to herself.

Someone watching the front of a bus as it approaches sees the face of a gentle, fatherly man.

A young woman says loudly into a cell phone, Yeah?

4

Tom lays Hettie's small red backpack, which has a picture of a school bus on it, with the letters of her name written in magic marker in each of its windows, into the sling seat of the stroller. She doesn't want to ride, she wants to push, and as they walk down East Broadway toward the bus stop he keeps his hand over hers on one of the down-curved handles, not to help her navigate—she's quite good at it—but for the contact.

Just as they are about to pass the entrance to Seward Park a girl, ten or eleven years old, runs through it and out onto the sidewalk, waving a badminton racket over her head. It isn't until she has turned and is running ahead of them that they can see she is chasing a squirrel. She is fast and the squirrel cannot enlarge the distance between them, about three feet, which is also the length of her arm and the racket combined: still the girl does not swing. Perhaps she knows it would require slowing down and that would allow the squirrel to gain the necessary distance to pass out of reach. Perhaps she doesn't really want to hurt the squirrel, just to enact the gesture of hurting it. When the squirrel leaps onto the trunk of an ailanthus tree she swings the racket at full force, and just misses as it scoots upward. By the time they pass her it has disappeared into the upper branches, but the girl hasn't stopped whacking the trunk with her racket.

After they have gotten off the bus, and are heading up the block toward the building they live in—Hettie, now tired, is riding in the stroller—they run into Hannie, a friend who lives nearby: a woman in her mid-thirties, a single mother of two daughters, one older than Hettie, one younger. It's unusual to see her without one or both of them. He asks after her mother, who he knows is gravely ill.

Hannie tells him she's on her way up to the Bronx, to look at a hospice that's been recommended to her by the physician treating her mother. This, though no one needs to say it, means that she is on her way to what will probably be the last place her mother will occupy in this life. Today, she will see it alone, as she most likely will again, after her mother has died. She looks down at Hettie, asleep in the stroller, leans over her, takes the sippy-cup from her hand and hands it to him. He can see how much of herself Hannie holds inside, not hidden, but contained: Through this season of her life everything her senses can perceive—this sidewalk, the plane passing high overhead, the turnstile she will soon push herself through at the subway station, all of it and everything else—will be, and will remain, pitilessly real. She will efficiently complete the tasks she is required to perform.

❖

Hettie, still napping, lies beside him on the couch. He writes in his notebook about the young woman in the bus shelter, more specifically how the force of gravity that had pulled his attention to her, that had held her in his thoughts, has been weakened by time, by the interposition of the things he saw and did in the two hours since he stood near her, and by the opposing pull of his own needs. He writes about speaking to Hannie on the street and how afterward, as he slowly climbed the stairs to their apartment carrying the stroller with his sleeping daughter, he felt, within the familiar chemistry of late-afternoon wooziness, the unsettling substance of helplessness.

Tom writes, now, that his daughter had woken up as he set her down on the couch—though she hadn't—because the intersession of her awakened presence was the next thing he wanted to have happen. He writes that upon waking she had asked for chocolate milk, an after-school ritual, and then asked him to read her the book that the teacher had been reading when he picked her up from school. In this version of the events following their arrival home, he first took from the shelf the one about the human parents whose child was a brontosaurus and she shook her head. It was the other one she wanted, in which the dinosaurs have a wild dance party that lasts until they fall asleep forever.

There is no more boring a subject, he writes, *than himself*.

Most of it adds up to this: Whatever he thinks he's writing about, he's always searching the appearances of other people in the hope of recognizing some aspect of the ever-present, familiar, unintelligible substance of what his own life feels like.

※

Sometime in the next half hour his wife, Joan, who like him is both a writer and a professor, will get home from the university where she teaches, his daughter will wake, and the vegetable dumplings, chicken in garlic sauce, and home-style tofu and vegetables he has just called to order for their dinner will be delivered.

As he waits he reads a story by one of his students that will be discussed tomorrow in workshop. Nick, the writer of the story, is from North Carolina. He was twenty-three, in veterinary school, and married for less than a year when his wife told him she had discovered that the life they'd planned to share was not the life she wanted to live. A few painful months after their separation, he accepted the fact that he probably felt the same way. He'd been writing stories since high school, though he'd never shown one to another living soul, and in this process of re-imagining his own life, he decided it was time. He had a quirky natural talent and after applying to more than a dozen graduate programs in creative writing, it turned out he had a choice and the choice he made, without hesitation, was for New York City and the university where Tom teaches.

※

Ginger, the main character of Nick's story, has just undergone a vicious divorce. Late one night she looks out the window of the house she'd once shared with her husband and now lives in alone, and sees a strange car parked in the driveway. As her eyes adjust to the darkness she sees her ex-husband making out with his new girlfriend in the front seat. Ginger, who is a plumber, grabs a four-foot length of steel pipe and runs outside.

The girlfriend, who is in the driver's seat, has kept the engine running, so that all she'd have to do in order to make a quick escape is pull the gear shift into reverse, and press the gas pedal to the floor. Even so, before the car speeds out of reach Ginger gets in one solid swing that pounds a spider-web pattern of smash-softened glass on the passenger side of the windshield, just inches from her ex-husband's face.

Ginger is the only plumber in town who takes late-night emergency calls, and later that night she finds two large Ziploc bags of PCP in a clogged toilet. The woman who called was crying. *An hour ago the cops arrested Rudy—he's only sixteen!—and now my bathroom is flooded.* Without telling the woman she hides the two bags in her toolbox.

Before going home, she stops at a twenty-four-hour supermarket where she buys two large steaks, then drives to her ex-husband's house, quietly gets out of the truck, crouches in front of the twelve-foot fence he'd erected because of the escalating violence that began during their divorce proceedings and has continued since, pours the entire contents of each bag of PCP onto the steaks, and hurls them over the fence to the two snarling Doberman Pinschers on the other side. This act of vengeance finally allows her to release enough of her anger toward her ex-husband and begin life anew by saying yes to her neighbor, who's been asking her to go out to dinner with him since the beginning of the story.

Tom writes a note on the last page of the manuscript: "I enjoyed reading this weird and engaging story, but felt it relies too much on its most immediate sense of conflict, the dramatic tit-for-tat nature of their fighting, rather than a more complex, less explicable sense of character. The story implies that the plumber has much more to her than meets the eye, but doesn't yet show it. Why not try to add a more personal sense of what it's like to be her while she's undergoing the transition of her divorce?"

❖

He turns on the news. The familiar newscaster with gray-white hair, who worked for this network during the last Iraq war and all the years between, appears on the screen, and when the sound comes up he's in the middle of a sentence, " . . . in southern Iraq, that killed seven civilians."

His image is replaced by footage of a white minivan pocked with lines of bullet holes, under spotlights that ignite the fringes of jagged glass edging the shot-out windows, and cause a dance of bright lines and circles in the camera's lens.

"A *Washington Post* reporter embedded with the Marines wrote, I quote, 'No warning shot was fired.'"

The words on the crawl sliding beneath him speak of the mayor's plans for heightened security along the Easter Parade route.

The bell rings. His daughter stirs in her sleep. He walks the length of their narrow floor-through apartment to the kitchen, to the buzzer that opens the door downstairs and just as he presses it the bell rings again. While the man delivering their dinner is climbing the stairs, he quickly walks back into the living room.

His daughter is now sitting up on the couch, watching the lead-in footage that precedes the commercial break: a parade balloon of Wile E. Coyote, drifting from side to side as it moves above a crowd lining Fifth Avenue. Music accompanies the footage, a pleasing, sturdy, soft male voice from his childhood—Eddie Fisher? Perry Como?—singing "In your Easter bonnet . . ."

5

After dinner, after Hettie has had her bath and gone to sleep, Tom sits beside Joan on the couch, watching her drink her third glass of wine. He has not done drugs in twenty years, not had a drink in nearly fifteen, yet watching Joan lift the glass to her lips, he envies her the taste and, even more so, the ability to alter sensation that he associates with that taste. He assumes that she wants to soften the effects of the world more than on those nights when she doesn't drink after supper, or at all. He recalls the woman he passed earlier on his walk to the bus stop, carrying all those bags of potato chips, and sees her broad, continuous, private smile. Her appearance was the reminder of what, for him, had been an illusory kind of control— no, not illusory: real, but short-lived—that he could actually summon a feeling he chose in advance, bring about a state of being he simultaneously desired and foresaw, and maintain it for the brief span of time before he got too high or too drunk to ask himself what he was feeling and receive a comprehensible answer.

He picks up the remote, aims it at the TV, but Joan begins to speak so he doesn't turn it on. She tells him about the argument that arose in her class today when two students announced that they planned to participate in a dramatic anti-war protest scheduled for Saturday night.

"They're going to dress up as waiters and waitresses, then approach people waiting on lines in front of theaters holding trays with dolls on them that are disfigured, burnt, and spattered with blood-red paint, and say 'Your order is ready.' They've already *borrowed* the trays from the cafeteria."

"Wow."

"At first, the argument was about tactics, about who you wanted or didn't want to alienate. But then it grew into a yelling match between students who actively opposed the war and those for whom, in their words, the whole thing—the president, shock and awe, the Coalition of the Willing—was bogus.

"One student asked why a heterosexist Pope is less bogus than Karl Rove or Britney Spears." Joan holds up her glass. "In one corner the opposition; in the other, those who believe everything in this world is bullshit to an equal degree."

She picks up the remote, presses the "on" button, and drops it back on the couch. "It's an argument," she says, "and it's *not* an argument at the same time."

The last moment of a commercial briefly appears on the screen: a golden retriever leaps into the air in slow motion, opens its mouth and catches a red Frisbee.

Then a news desk beneath a row of network images appears, but is quickly replaced by the chalky black-and-white footage, transmitted from a camera mounted in the nose cone of a Tomahawk missile, playing on the screen of a video monitor set on the center of a stage. Beside it, a military spokesman in desert camouflage, speaking in a steady, authoritative, reassuring voice like that of an airline pilot is reminding a room filled with reporters somewhere in Qatar, as well as the audience watching at home, of the careful planning and thorough intelligence involved in the selection of targets. The missile's footage pauses, freezing time in the moment before impact, so that the spokesman, using a pointer, can indicate a set of four short equal lines, formed like crosshairs with the middle erased, creating instead, at the point they'd intersect, a circle, though an imagined one: a bull's eye not located on the target that hovers just beneath—the shadowy tops of two attached buildings—but in the point of a weapon so arrogantly precise it cannot miss. The footage resumes. Without a sound the target is pulled upward into the circle. The image disappears: The camera is obliterated in the same instant the two structures are demolished.

Then another quick cut to the news desk, followed by a replay of the reporter embedded with the Seventh Armored Division, from whose mouth comes an even more edited-down version of the report he filed that morning, though enough still remains for him to once again warn the Iraqis about the strength of coalition forces and again repeat the phrase "steel wave."

Tom points to the screen. "This morning that guy mixed up Desert Storm with Operation Iraqi Freedom."

"A bogus name is as slippery as any other kind of lie."

The footage of the white bullet-riddled minivan Tom had watched earlier appears again and in this segment the quote from the *Washington Post* reporter has been replaced by a quote from a military spokesman who says that none of the Marines at the checkpoint know why the driver of the van hadn't stopped after they fired warning shots.

"Fuck," he says to Joan. "*Fucking* fucks."

"What?"

"They changed it. Now they're blaming the people they killed."

"It *is* bogus," Joan says.

"You've had enough to drink."

"I said that without irony."

"That something self-evidently what it is can be called something else. . . . And in that fucking tone of voice that implies, *we're certain you all agree*. . . . That's not bogus. That's a kind of violence." He's not sure if he's making sense. "In this cesspool you can't say anything without irony."

"We're all José Arcadio Segundo," Joan says, "all two hundred eighty-six million of us."

"What are you talking about?"

"García Márquez. *One Hundred Years of Solitude*."

"I haven't read it since I was a student."

"You should read it again," she says. "It's the one book I include each year in the novel survey course."

"I want a drink," he says.

"Remember when he saw the soldiers kill thousands of people and take their bodies away on trains and he was the only one who survived?"

"Who?" He's annoyed at his wife because she doesn't seem as frightened as he is at the moment, and because she can drink, even get drunk if she wants to, while he cannot.

"José Arcadio Segundo . . . and then over time, after years of

37

being the only one who remembered, he finally begins to doubt his own memory, too? Don't you remember?"

He picks up the remote and blackens the TV screen. "Let's leave this fucking thing off till the end of the decade."

※

After Joan has gone to bed, he sits at the kitchen table, leafing through her marked-up paperback copy of *One Hundred Years of Solitude*. As he scans the pages, he searches his own memory for that moment he experienced years ago as a reader and, seeing the familiar words and passages and names, he steps deeper and deeper back into the book, and by the time he finds the words themselves he has already re-envisioned nearly all of it.

José Arcadio Segundo, a citizen of Macondo, witnesses the murder of three thousand unarmed men, women, and children gathered at a train station, by soldiers who hold them under the steady fire of fourteen machine guns until no one stirs. He awakes later, bloody from a flesh wound, in one of two hundred train cars being carried toward the sea by three locomotives. After struggling through the cars, all of them filled with corpses, he reaches the back of the train, jumps off, and, walking back along the tracks, he reaches Macondo. In the first house he goes to, a woman gives him a cup of coffee. After he tells her about what's happened, and what he has seen, she informs him that no one has died, and that nothing like this has happened in Macondo for many years, not since the time of his uncle the colonel. And after that, when he goes to the square beside the station, he can find no trace of the massacre.

Tom, inside the dream of fiction, witnessed both this terrible act of violence, and watched the invasive process of historical revision begin to bore like a worm into the memory of a single person. It took years before José Arcadio began to doubt what he'd seen. In the dream of this world, the one outside the dream of fiction, it can take less than a single day.

He is surprised at how re-reading these pages gives him a kind of relief. Perhaps that relief resides in the fact that Gabriel García Márquez has imagined a shape for such an experience that, without much tailoring, can be altered to fit the current historical moment: a form for such despair which can be measured, perhaps framed in time—even, possibly, given a name.

Again

March 22–23

What has happened before can happen again. So can what hasn't.
—Bertolt Brecht

"We have made clear the doctrine which says, if you harbor a terrorist, if you feed a terrorist, if you hide a terrorist, you're just as guilty as the terrorist. We're holding regimes responsible for harboring and supporting terror."
—President George W. Bush, 9/10/03

They don't use words to speak. They use them to stop thought.
—Christopher Baughman

6

Because she has her eyes closed, the woman sitting across from Tom on the subway, rocking to the music pouring into her head through earbuds, doesn't notice him studying her each time he looks up at her from the lines of words he's scribbling in his notebook. He had the idea that if he described her quickly, while in her presence, his representation of her would be less subject to the ways he inadvertently shapes what he sees while in the process of remembering. He wants the words containing how he sees her to add up to a person less familiar, less comprehensible, less his.

For him, however, even after all the years of writing in notebooks, the act of composing words about people while in their presence is a new experience. He doesn't feel like a painter shifting his gaze from canvas to model and back again, he feels like someone staring down the blouse of a woman leaning over to tie her shoe. Nearly each time he looks at the woman, he glances sideways, quickly, at the other seven or eight people in the car: as far as he can tell, none of them show any interest in what he is doing.

It's Saturday. Joan's in her office at school, where she can concentrate on her own writing, and Hettie's at home with a babysitter. He intended to work on a story that would somehow include the two guys and the smiling woman with the potato chips he'd passed on his way to the bus stop yesterday, the young woman speaking on the cell phone and his imagined version of who she was talking to and what she was talking about, and a girl chasing a squirrel with a badminton racquet. The story would also include a short step back in time, to a character sitting on a stoop on St. Marks Place writing in his notebook and, from there, another short step backward to the experience that character was writing about: standing on First Avenue with his daughter as a film crew prepares to shoot a scene.

After working on this story for two hours, or trying to, he decided to visit the Museum of Modern Art. It wasn't just the difficulty of conceiving the shape of a story that could include all of that, it was also the fact that, since Hettie was born, he has come to inhabit time differently. First its passage slowed down, attaching itself to the slower pace at which his new daughter experienced it. And now, his days so crammed with family as well as teaching, when he finds himself in sole possession of a short span of time he becomes anxious and uncertain about how to make the best use of it, so much so that he often does nothing at all. Consequently, most of what he's written in the last four years, he has written in notebooks. Joan, however, in spite of the added demands a young child places on a mother, had been able to complete the novel she'd started while she was pregnant and is already well into a new one. She had advised him to write something longer, so that after leaving for a time to do the things a busy life required, he'd have a place to return to.

✹

A woman he knew years ago, when he first stopped drinking, and who had lived with him for nearly a month, had told him that spending time in the permanent collection in the Museum of Modern Art had a healing effect. She had gone to art school but dropped out in her third year. At the twelve-step meeting where they met, she had said that one source of the depression that had brought about her excessive drinking was the fact that the golden age of visual arts had come and gone. There was nothing a living artist could do, or perhaps would ever be able to do, to top what had been done in the first half of the twentieth century. Though it had been the source of her despair, she later discovered that being in the presence of modern art was also what would help her recover. The invention and discovery, the boldness and color, the firm belief that creating *and* experiencing a work of art could actually change the way we think—even if it meant dreaming the dream of another era, that was where she needed to live.

One morning, while sharing at a meeting, she broke into tears. The landlord of the building in which she'd been living for the past two years had discovered that she was subletting illegally. That much she knew. But what she hadn't known, until that day, was that the man she was subletting from, who'd been her boyfriend for a time when they were both students at Cooper Union, had been paying only two hundred and sixty dollars per month on a lease that dated back to the days of rent control, while charging her seven hundred and fifty.

The effect of being evicted could be devastating to anyone, but especially someone newly sober. So he invited her to stay with him until she could find a new place to live. Though the intention was that she'd be sleeping on the fold-out couch on the opposite end of the apartment—it was unwise, they'd both been told, to enter a new relationship during the first ninety days of sobriety—they ended up sharing a bed the second night, and nearly every night of her residency, before she decided to return to Los Angeles where she'd grown up. At twelve-step meetings people are known only by the first name they introduce themselves with each time they speak—hers was Nibor—and he knew her by no other name. She never told him what her last name was, never received a letter or a phone call during the short time they'd lived together, and it never occurred to him to ask. But nearly a year after she left she received an official-looking letter at his address with what he assumed was her entire name behind the clear address window: Evelyn Nibor Whalen. And over the months following she received two more: each with different first names, though the middle and last names were the same.

At least twice each week, during the time she lived in his apartment, they took the subway uptown to the museum, and together they walked around the permanent collection. About its healing effects she was absolutely right. She had told him that being there was the only thing in adult life that, for her, could compare to the nights she'd spent looking out the window of the bedroom she slept in as a child. She refused to explain it further, and he was glad she hadn't. The works of Giacometti and Ernst and Duchamp are public declarations that even the most silent of words, whispered in the remotest corners of our inner lives, can be given a form in which it can be spoken aloud. What could be more pleasurable, exciting, and reasonable than spending time in their presence? How could such an activity not have the power to heal? Their walks together through the galleries filled with paintings and objects are a gift he remains grateful for.

He has not gone to a meeting in more than a dozen years, though there are days on which he knows he should. On such days—and today is one—if he has the rare combination of the time and the presence of mind to do such a thing with it, he visits the permanent collection. However, today, when he arrived at the museum, he found both sides of the building enclosed in a plywood barrier, much of it covered with posters for films, pop music albums, graffiti, and announcements for anti-war rallies that have already happened or have yet to. He'd forgotten that the Museum of Modern Art was undergoing renovation and would not reopen until sometime next year.

On the barrier in front of the places where the entrances had been were small framed signs with a message describing the renovation in progress. After reading one, he stepped back and looked at the four-by-eight sheet of plywood it was attached to as if the sign had been one of the plaques set on the museum walls beside the works of art. He projected onto it the anticipation he'd carried with him on the subway ride uptown: clear images of the paintings and sculptures, or parts of them, and the long-shot possibility of coming across Nibor, standing before Chagall's *I and the Village*. Each time he stood beside her, staring into the seamless, embrangled medley of people and clouds and animals and sky, he was transported into a place where a body made of light and color can pass without hindrance into another body, as freely as the eye of memory can enter the eye that sees the world really there.

❖

A woman gets on at Rockefeller Plaza, sits at the end of the long seat he's in the middle of, and after quickly scanning the car, holds her gaze on him. As he continues writing in his notebook, periodically looking up at the woman across from him, whose eyes are still closed, he feels this new passenger's gaze intensify and focus into an accusation. And though the beam of the stare radiating from this woman could not reach the words he is writing, he turns to a new page, and on it he lists the names of the sculptures and paintings he'd looked forward to seeing on his earlier subway ride uptown to the museum. In doing so, in performing this ridiculous personal act of self-conscious behavior modification, he adds brief comments, as if he had just seen them and is inscribing his new responses on the plaques he imagines on the walls beside them.

Broadway Boogie Woogie, Piet Mondrian. Still powerful for more reasons than I know.

The Lacemakers (Les Broudouses), Vuillard. Still one of my favorites.

Fur-Lined Cup and Saucer (Le Dejeuner en fourrure), Meret Oppenheim. My dear old friend and favorite surrealist object, your fur is becoming a little threadbare.

In writing this last note he loses awareness of the woman watching him and remembers standing with Hettie in front of three antelopes in one of the dioramas at the Museum of Natural History and discovering that, in the decades since his own childhood visits with his father, their fur has thinned out and acquired the look of worn upholstery. There were two adult antelopes and a young one with its head poked under the long torso of the female, nursing. They stood on a grassy plot of earth beside a tree. Small birds were feeding at their feet. Behind them was a painted wall of distant mountains.

Pointing at the three inanimate creatures, Hettie had asked, "Which one are you?"

Lunar Asparagus, Max Ernst. I like it much better today than before.

The Music Lesson, Henri Matisse. *I used to love this one, and maybe still do, but today it felt too familiar, too much like a dream I can interpret too easily. Maybe that's because it's on so many postcards.*

❋

The train reaches the 23rd Street station. Four more stops before he gets off. He turns and smiles at the woman who'd been watching him and still is, and, mysteriously, she smiles back.

He turns forward, stares brazenly at the woman seated across from him, flips back to his description of her and reads what he wrote:

Forty or so, dark-skinned, a red wool bowl-shaped cap swelled with a dome of hair. Tattooed in blue ink on the knuckle at the base of each thumb is a small and perfect circle the size of the hole in a vinyl record, or an "o" written between the ruled lines of a notebook. Silver bands, as wide as Band-Aids, on the ring-, middle-, and forefinger of her left hand, which rests, palm downward, across the soft top of the black leather bag on her lap that is sending out, from its unzipped top, the wire bearing the music which rises in a straight ink-thin line, splits into a Y just below her chin, climbs into the bottom of her cap. Her leg rises and falls, bends at the knee, her foot bouncing, toe and heel, toe and heel, like a drummer pedaling a steady beat-line into a high-hat cymbal. Her eyes held tightly shut.

❋

When the train comes to a stop at the 14th Street station, he looks away from her and adds, in preparation for a story he might, later, write:

She opened her eyes then, for the first time since he got on the train, reached under her cap, removed the earbuds, smiled at him, stood, crossed the width of the car, sat beside him and asked, "Will you show me what you wrote?"

❋

Walking through the living room, he pauses behind the couch on which his daughter and Ayo, her babysitter, have fallen asleep. A spoon in one hand, the bowl of pea soup he's just reheated in the microwave palmed in the other, he watches the TV, which is still on, mostly to listen to the energetic version of "I'm a Believer" that accompanies the last scene and the credits of the movie Shrek, which they must have been watching before they fell asleep. When the spoon breaks the surface of the soup, a cloudlet of rich steam reaches his nose. He brings a spoonful to his mouth; the tape clicks to a stop: His tongue discovers that a marble-sized core of soup has remained as cold as an ice cube, and the image on the screen is replaced by a nurse, in green scrubs, looking into the eyes of a doctor, a surgical mask hung loosely around his neck, to whom she is saying, with evident affection, "It takes one to know one."

He is struck by the feeling that this has happened to him before, yet immediately following that feeling is the awareness that it has not. Instead, something has leapt out of the past, and joined itself to the present like the fur wedded to the china on Meret Oppenheim's cup and saucer. That, likewise, had been a moment possessed of a profound sense of both unpredictability and coincidence. For some reason he is certain of this, and certain that the two moments, occurring in their different regions of time, have nothing else in common. Even so, his first instinct is to turn and look backwards, to watch the thread disappear into the underbrush: and though it is a sucker's game, he can't *not* believe that the *first thing* holds an answer—so crawls in after it.

He emerges in a small cabin at a writers' colony in the Berkshire Mountains. This is ten years ago, just before he met Joan: A black ant is scurrying across the small table that serves as his desk. With one hand he sweeps it carefully into the other, opens the screen door, hurls it out, and actually sees—though he hadn't realized it until his heart commenced its next beat—its tri-orbed body collide with a bumblebee, hovering in the space that had been empty when his arm began its upward swing.

He turns off the TV and gives the soup another sixty seconds in the microwave. On his way to his desk, walking past the couch where Hettie and Ayo are still asleep, one more incident realizes itself in his mind. It occurred the day before Hettie was born. Joan had suggested he get an additional package of disposable diapers for newborns in case they were so busy in the first weeks after the birth that running such errands would prove difficult.

He was on the check-out line in a supermarket a few blocks from their apartment with two items in his cart: a package of seventy-two diapers and a sippy-cup with a picture of Dora the Explorer on it. He didn't yet know who that was, but he assumed—correctly as it turned out—that he would, by the time his daughter was old enough to drink out of it. As he waited, he was thinking that the apartment he would soon bring these diapers back to, in which there already were three other large packages of the same diapers, would be his daughter's first home, and all the things in it—the walls, furniture, windowsills, doorknobs, lamp shades, dusty undersides of chairs and beds—would all fix themselves in her memory from a perspective entirely unimaginable to him or Joan.

As he was thinking about this, he discovered that the woman on line in front of him and the woman directly behind him were identical twins. In his most recent book, which is dedicated to Hettie, there's a poem about this experience.

⁂

If the events of today—the visit to the museum, and everything that followed—could be gathered together within the shape of a story, he would end it with that poem.

Again

The cashier, holding down the key
so it repeatedly registers the same
price, says to the woman buying

twelve large cans of peeled tomatoes,
*It's been a little better since
he started using the foot bath.*

I'm next in line. I set my groceries
onto the belted counter, watching
the cashier pack the cans, six each,

into two double-thick plastic bags.
The woman then points toward
the cashier, but says to someone

behind me, *Didn't I tell her
it would work for him?* When I turn
I see the same woman: her twin.

Both are in their sixties, both
wear their short hair combed stiffly
back, and dyed the same golden red.

I turn to the first woman, then quickly
back to the second, who is smiling
now, and who says, *He thinks he's drunk,*

and the two begin to laugh. *Don't worry,*
the cashier tells me, *This happens all
the time.* I am stricken, breathless,

ascendant: it's not that they're twins,
not even that I find myself standing
between them like Icarus between

his duplicate wings, it's how certain
I suddenly am that this has happened
before. Their twin-ness *not* the cause,

but my startled apprehension of it:
Again?—the first word to realize
itself—*Again*. The sister behind

me is waving now, *Hel-lo?* And I notice
that behind my groceries, which have
been conveyed to the cashier, are twelve

more cans of peeled tomatoes. She smiles
at the double-coincidence—I imagine
she is used to being regarded with the deep

and curious amazement only an identical
twin can cause—and by way of
explanation says, *They're on sale*.

7

Sunday morning. Tom and Hettie, having spent the last hour in Washington Square Park, are walking home. It's chilly, and there were few children in the park and none, other than Hettie, playing in the sand area because the sand, just beneath the surface, was still damp from yesterday's rain. Hettie, using a plastic shovel and bucket, made a wide, uneven circle of nuclear reactor-shaped sand cakes, spaced no more than a foot from each other. When the circle, ten or twelve feet in diameter, was complete, they collected twigs that fell from the branches of the sycamores stretching over the playground and planted them in the centers of the round flat tops of each mound.

❀

A crowd is gathered on the sidewalk of the block before theirs. From a distance it looks like a store-front gallery opening or people waiting to get into a club or, more likely on a Sunday morning, an open casting call for one of the off-off Broadway theaters on East Fourth Street.

Hettie, in a rush to find out what's going on, tugs his arm. But as they approach she grows confused, then disappointed, and when they're standing among the people—adults, mostly younger, lining the sidewalk in front of the double-wide building that used to be the Daughters of Bethlehem Home for Handicapped Children, talking in groups of two or three or into cell phones—she looks at them suspiciously. What are they all doing here if nothing's happening?

Her gaze settles on a woman at the far side of the line of people, holding a thin sheaf of fliers and pointing to the front of the building. He realizes, looking at the clean, bubblegum-pink brick, that this had been one of the last buildings in the neighborhood to still have the coal soot-darkened walls that are the thumbprint of the nineteenth century. He hadn't noticed they'd been sandblasted—

has it been six months? two years?—and now he sees the clear, new panes between the old wooden sashes on the curtainless windows, and through them the clean white walls of the empty rooms. It's an open house, a first look for the people gathered here, some of whom may become tenants in the condos or co-ops that will be the internal organs of the building's new anatomy.

His daughter holds her focus on the woman who, in her eyes, must be the reason everyone has come. She's wearing a tailored business suit but no overcoat, though the air is cold and damp. She is strikingly beautiful, barely older than a teenager, and has the self-assured corporate manner of the newscasters Joan refers to as anchor bunnies. She stands where the teachers and attendants often stood, and the people crowding the sidewalk are waiting where the children, Tom remembers, would assemble and form a line before walking to the park, or boarding a school bus for a day trip.

Tom had first moved into their apartment as a student, more than twenty-five years ago, and in his comings and goings the sight of the children, entering or leaving the building, out in the neighborhood in small groups with some of their teachers, had long been familiar. Again he sees their awkward movements, their faces and bodies and speech shaped by the various conditions they suffered from. Were they here now, his daughter would not mask her stare as adults have learned to do.

He hears his name called. He turns toward the voice, sees a man he doesn't recognize further up the line calling his name again and pointing at himself. Tom approaches, holding Hettie's hand. The man, about his age, is wearing a Columbia University sweatshirt, jeans, and white jogging sneakers.

Tom looks at the round, smiling face, the thick, dark, youthful hair, and still he doesn't recognize this man.

"*Jim*-my," the man says.

"Jimmy?" Tom says back.

"*Jim*-my," the man says. "DelVecchio."

"You?" he says to the man, then, "Here?"

"In the flesh. How long has it been?"

"Thirty years. No, more. Jeez. More than thirty years. How are you? What are you doing here?"

"Same as everyone else." He holds up the prospectus sheets for the apartments. "You, too?"

"No. We live on the next block."

In their senior year of high school Jimmy DelVecchio had changed the spelling of his name to Jimi, in honor of Jimi Hendrix, and began pronouncing it with added stress on the first syllable so that it would be possible to hear the changed spelling in his voice. It soon caught on and everyone pronounced it that way. It was even spelled that way in the yearbook.

"No shit. Then"—Jimi points to the building—"we could soon be neighbors?" He shakes his head and, in the language of their old neighborhood, adds, "Tommy, I ain't believin this." He then looks down at Hettie, gesturing with dramatic surprise, as if he's just noticed she was there. "And who are you?"

She takes a half step behind Tom.

Jimi kneels in front of her and she moves further behind him. "What's your name?"

She looks over his head and says nothing.

"How old are you?"

Still nothing. Even adults she knows and likes do not get answers to such questions. Looking down, watching his daughter and Jimi, he sees a reddish-brown tinge in Jimi's hair that wasn't there when they were in high school.

Jimi tells Hettie that he has two children, a boy and a girl. He then rises to his feet. "They're both going to Columbia. Or will soon. My daughter's in her first year at the law school. My son'll be a freshman next year. That's why we're looking to move back. To be near the kids."

"From where?"

"The company sent me to D.C. eighteen years ago."

"Compared to where we grew up," Tom says to Jimi, "this is hardly *back*."

"It's back for someone living where *I've* been living. Not that we don't love it there. We do. And the house the kids grew up in, it's enormous." He points at the prospectus, tilts his head toward the building. "There's a lot of equity to flip over into this."

Every Friday during the spring of their last year of high school, recruiters of different kinds came to do presentations at the seniors-only assembly. They were from different branches of the military, the police department, offices of state and federal civil services, Wall Street investment firms, and other corporations. In 1970, the year they graduated, less than a third of those who completed their high school educations would go on to college. Jimi signed up for an entry-level position in an investment banking firm. Most of the jobs and military stints didn't begin until the end of summer, allowing them to complete one last season in their school-life cycle before crossing the border into adulthood. He hasn't seen Jimi since that summer following their graduation.

When they were seventeen Jimi was funny, handsome, and mischievous. He had the grace of someone with the stature and appearance of a grown-up, while in full possession of the lambent irreverence and blind courage of a teenager. Tom remembers one of the first warm afternoons of the spring of their senior year, when he and Jimi and three other guys snuck out of school at lunchtime and drove to White Castle in Johnny LaGerscio's car. The radio volume was turned as high as it would go. Though all the windows were open, the car smelled of English Leather and the Marlboros all five of them would light up after flicking the ones smoked down to their filters out into the bright, barely visible world they were driving through.

He was in the back seat between Joe Lazarro and Jimmy Fitzgerald. Jimi rode shotgun with Johnny. At one point, when they were stopped at a light, Jimi reached over, turned off the ignition, and pulled out the key.

"Give me that," Johnny said, laughing. They were all laughing.

"Not till you say your mother's a whore," Jimi said.

The light changed. They were all laughing hysterically now. Someone behind them honked and without saying a word Joe and Jimmy each reached their arms, middle fingers raised, out the back windows.

"C'mon," Johnny said, getting annoyed.

"Not till you say it. Your mother's a whore."

When Johnny reached for the keys, Jimi threw them past him and out the driver's-side window into the weeds bursting through the broken pavement on the narrow traffic island.

Johnny got out and picked them up, got back into the driver's seat, pretended to hand the keys back to Jimi, then slid them into the ignition and started the car. Meanwhile the light had changed back to red again.

While they were waiting Jimi said to Johnny, "I'm sorry. I know your mother's not a whore. I mean"—here he turned to the three of them in the back seat—"I don't know about you guys, but she never asked me for a dime."

❖

Hettie walks over to the woman holding the leaflets. She hands her one, points over her head at Tom and says, "This is for your daddy."

"One for me," Hettie says.

"Just one," the woman tells her. Hettie remains there, standing in front of her, and pretends to read the words and numbers.

"I heard that you're a writer." Jimi says. "And some kind of professor?"

"I am."

"What do you write about?"

"That's hard to answer. At the moment I'm writing about our lives, here, now, during this war." He doesn't know why he's telling him this. It's certainly not because it's true. "Not doing a great job, though."

"Maybe because there isn't much to write about. How many ways can you say, We're really kicking their ass, and, It'll be over in less than a month?"

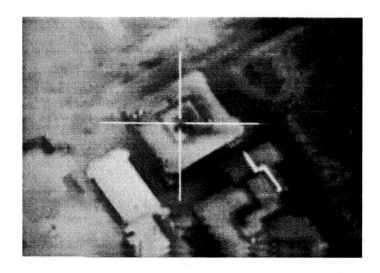

He's surprised at Jimi's easy certainty, and the apparent pleasure it offered him to say what he'd just said. Surprised, too, that Jimi assumes he shares his feelings, that they are both part of a gloating unanimous "we" who are all somehow in on the ass-kicking.

"It won't be like Vietnam," Jimi says. "They'll all be home before they get any older."

"Excuse me," Tom looks toward Hettie; the young woman, still talking to her, smiles at him and says, "We're having a chat."

"You hear anything lately about Johnny?" Jimi asks him.

The fall following their high school graduation the draft lottery had its first round of annual selections. Of the five boys sitting in the car that afternoon, he and Jimi would be the only two with numbers high enough to avoid service. Jimmy Fitzgerald, once he got his number, joined the navy, hoping to avoid combat duty. Joe Lazarro opted for artillery school. Johnny LaGerscio followed the route the army laid out for those who made no choices prior to induction, and became an infantryman. He lost both legs, just below the thigh, when he stepped on a land mine.

"The last I heard," Jimi says, "he moved to Virginia with his parents. That was ten, maybe twelve years ago."

"I think we have to go," he says to Jimi, and walks toward the woman, who is no longer talking to his daughter but to a young couple who are prospective buyers.

As he approaches he is struck again by the young woman's beauty, yet also how her adult bearing seems overstated and awkward, like a child wearing her mother's clothing.

"I'm told it had once been an orphanage," she says to the couple, who smile, turn, and nod thoughtfully. He takes Hettie's hand.

"Actually," Tom tells the woman, and the couple, as well, "it was a home for handicapped children."

Jimi is standing beside them now. He hands Tom a business card, takes it back, writes down a cell phone number, and then hands it to him again. He still spells his first name *Jimi*. "If we actually become neighbors again . . . Am I believin that? It would be so cool."

"I don't have a card," he says.

Jimi pulls a cell phone out of the pouch pocket in the front of his sweatshirt, flips it open, and says, "Okay."

"What?"

"He wants your phone number," the woman who is part of the couple says.

He recites it to Jimi. Then they all remain silent for a moment while Jimi programs the number into his phone with his thumbs.

When he finishes, Hettie begins to tug on Tom's arm.

"It's time to go," he says, as if they've been in a longer conversation than they actually have.

"Do you think it's haunted?" the woman standing beside her husband asks him.

Tom knows she's talking to him, but doesn't get what she is saying.

The beautiful real estate agent says, "Do you?"

Jimi, smiling, leans further into the conversation.

"Do I what?" Tom says.

She points to the front of the building. "Think it's haunted?"

He looks at the building, then back at the beautiful woman and says, "No. But I think it's about to be."

8

"Smoke," Hettie says suddenly. They have just reached the corner of Second Avenue and are waiting for the light to change.

"Smoke?" Tom looks across the street, and up and down the avenue to see if anything is burning. "Where?"

She points to a woman trying to cross the avenue diagonally and against the light, who has been stopped, halfway, by a passing bus.

The light changes and, as they begin to cross, the woman his daughter had pointed to shouts "Hey" and walks quickly toward a policewoman standing in front of a blue SUV with a six-foot aluminum ladder strapped onto its roof rack. "It's Sunday."

As they near her, he sees that it's the same woman who was standing behind them in the crowd last Saturday as they watched the film crew prepare to shoot the scene in the taxi, the woman who continued talking as she repeatedly inhaled and exhaled smoke. She's wearing a leather tool belt, though all the holster loops are empty except one in which she's carrying a long, paint-spattered flathead screwdriver.

The policewoman has not looked back at her.

"It's fuckin Sunday," she says to her, shouting, even though she's standing beside her.

"Thank you," the police officer tells her, in a Caribbean accent. "I knew that."

"Then why are you writing me a goddamn ticket?"

Neither of the two seems aware that he and his daughter, having crossed to their side, have stopped just a few feet away to watch them. He is certain that Hettie, holding his hand, is feeling a version of the same thing he is: that they are experiencing a change-your-partner recombination of the moment, a week before, when the three of them were watching the two actors in the taxi rehearse the scene.

"Your inspection sticker. It expired a week ago."

"Damn," the woman says. She turns toward him and his daughter, though she doesn't appear to recognize them, then looks around to see if anyone else is watching. "I'm on the job seven days a week. When do I have time?"

The policewoman, finished writing, rips off the ticket, an envelope, colored the same orange and white as a Creamsicle, with the summons she has written attached at a serrated-edge fold. She steps onto the sidewalk, lifts the wiper blade on the driver's side of the windshield and slips it underneath. "I'll leave this here then," she says. "If you leave it, too, you won't get another summons today."

As they approach their apartment building they meet Hannie, who is kneeling before her stroller with her back to him and his daughter, pulling a mitten onto the hand of Jolie, who is sixteen months old. Violet, the nine-year-old sister, with one hand on the stroller's handle, stands as far away from it as the length of her arm will allow, hums, sleepy and bored, looks down at the sidewalk, and sways slowly back and forth.

Hettie walks up to them first and places herself close beside Hannie to see what she's doing. Hannie leans over and gives her a peck on the cheek while she reaches into her own coat pocket, removes a second mitten, and slips it over Jolie's other hand. When she has finished, Hettie gives her the prospectus sheet she has carried home.

Hannie stands up again and reads it aloud. "Two bedrooms, two baths, living/dining room, kitchen, breakfast nook, eight hundred twenty-five thousand dollars." She hands it back to his daughter, then looks at him with a small, sly smile on her face. "Don't tell me you guys are moving."

"No," he tells her, "but we'll all be getting some new neighbors."

She reads the address on the top of the sheet and nods her head in the general direction of the building. "If I need a corporate lawyer or a liposuctionist, I'll know where to go." Then she says, "They're moving my mother on Tuesday."

"I don't teach that day," he says, anticipating her need for assistance.

"Jolie's in daycare," she says, then points at her older daughter. "But Violet's in a play that afternoon."

Violet does not lift her eyes. She has stopped humming, but continues swaying.

"She wants to come with me," her mother says. "She's a big girl and she wants to help."

"Ma," Violet says, whiney and dreamy. "It's a dumb play."

"You've worked so hard," Hannie says to her, "learning all those lines." She then turns to Tom. "She practically memorized the whole play. She's playing two parts and she made her own costumes."

"What's the name of it," he asks.

"*A Midsummer Night's Dream*."

"I like that one." He points to his daughter. "And she'd love to see it, too."

"It's not even summer," Violet says. "It's still cold out. Why do I have to be in that stupid shitty play."

"Violet?" Hannie says.

"*Two* parts," he says. "Wow. Which ones?"

"A dumb fairy?" she says. "And the lady who gets married at the end?"

"Hippolyta?"

She doesn't answer.

"Yup," Hannie says, and then adds, "She's the only one in the whole play with two parts. We're going over to K-Mart now to get some green hair dye, the kind that washes out."

"We'll applaud from the audience," he says. He claps his hands. Then he kneels down and tries to get Hettie to clap, too, but she stops when he stops moving his hands.

"It's at three-fifteen," Hannie says.

"We'll be there," he says. "We'll clap the loudest. Then we'll bring you home. And tell your mother all about it."

After he has taken off Hettie's coat and sweater and laid them on a kitchen chair, she climbs onto her step-stool in front of the sink. He squirts liquid Ivory soap onto her hands and, as she rubs them together under the water falling from the tap, it occurs to him that she's being unusually cooperative. More often than not he has to wrestle with her to take off her coat and shoes, and then argue for ten minutes before she'll wash her hands. When she can, Joan spends Sundays at her office at school, working on her own fiction. Though she has a desk in a corner at home, even a screen shielding it from view, their apartment isn't large enough for anyone to enjoy truly solitary concentration. When Hettie is home, even if she is with him or a babysitter, Joan cannot work for long without interruption.

After Hettie steps down and he dries her hands, she walks out of the kitchen, stops briefly to look into the bathroom, then continues on her way to the front end of the apartment and looks out the living room windows toward the buildings across the street. He senses in these actions some combination of feeling and motivation that includes first making sure her mother hasn't decided to come home early (and thus be found somewhere in the apartment), and then, ruling that out, attempting to detect her presence in the outside world she walked into earlier and will return from sometime later.

He stands beside her at the window. Now hovering between them and the sun is a dense cluster of clouds, and as they stare at the darkening windows across the street he wonders if Hettie noticed what he noticed earlier about the woman who got the ticket. Though she was as angry as she had been last week when she stood behind them in the crowd on First Avenue, smoking and talking, now she also seemed tired, helplessly so, and sad, like a child trying not to cry.

After a minute Hettie walks back to the couch, sits, and faces the TV. This means she'd like him to slip a tape into the VCR. It's too early in the day for her to watch a movie, but he's tired, wants to spend a moment with his notebook, and it's easier than actively entertaining her for the next hour or so.

"*Shrek?*" he asks her.

She lifts the remote from the coffee table and hands it to him.

Once she is settled he walks to the kitchen, sets his notebook and pen on the table, but then remembers to make their lunch. A peanut butter and jelly sandwich for her, peanut butter for him.

In the last few days he's been thinking about the twins he encountered in the supermarket more than three years ago. During the next year, the first year of Hettie's life, he had passed them on the street twice, and both times they were together. They never spoke to him or in any way acknowledged that they'd seen him before, which seemed perfectly normal, especially in a constantly changing neighborhood, filled with busy shops and tourists, where most people you see in public you see only once, and consequently have come to expect that the people you do know, even those you've known for decades, will be the rarer sight. He's seen them since those first two times, but never together, and he wonders, after each encounter, if he's just seen the one he saw the time before— his first, automatic-default assumption—or if it's the other of the two, or if, after so many years of inseparability they stopped getting along, or if one of them has moved away or died. Each time he hopes that the next time he'll see them together again and the mystery, or much of it, will be solved.

He slices the crust off his daughter's sandwich and, as he's cutting it in quarters, he hears Hettie's footsteps approach him, and stop. After a moment he hears her open the bathroom door.

"Need any help?" he shouts.

No answer. No water running. No toilet flushing. She is quiet. He gets up, walks toward the bathroom. She walks out just before he gets there, carrying their point-and-shoot camera.

"What are you doing with that?" he asks.

"It was in there," she says.

He follows her back to the living room. "Did you do anything with the camera?"

She sets it on the coffee table. "I took it in here."

"Do you want to keep watching the movie?" he asks, and points at the screen, but Hettie is already absorbed: it's one of her favorite scenes. The ogre Shrek and Princess Fiona are walking through a forest. Shrek catches a frog, blows air into its mouth until it has swelled like a balloon, ties a string to it, and gives it to her. Princess Fiona reciprocates by catching a snake, blowing it up, twisting it into the shape of a dog, and handing it to him.

He walks back to the bathroom and finds no evidence of anything amiss. Since he's in there he decides to urinate. When he leaves he closes the door tightly. There is no other sound in the apartment except the movie's soundtrack coming from the living room.

When he returns again to the kitchen he sees that the red light on the telephone that sits on the counter just inside the door is blinking. When they came in earlier he hadn't noticed.

"This is Jimi, your almost-new neighbor, looking out the window of a two-bedroom, two-bath apartment I'm about to make an offer on. Is it a small world or what? Wait, I wouldn't just be your *new* neighbor, I'd be your old *and* new neighbor. Remember what Ralphie used to say? I'm *so* stoned I actually think I'm *here* with the rest of you doofuses. Well, I am, and I'm happy about it. *Maron*, your neighbor again? Would that be a piss, or what?"

He continues listening. Not to the words themselves, but to Jimi's voice speaking the dead language of their adolescence. It's an idiom now foreign to him, and probably to Jimi, too, though Jimi is still willing to use it, at least with him, as the adhesive substance that could reunite them after so many years. Earlier on the street, as Jimi was going on and on with energy and enthusiasm, he mostly remained silent. Even now, his half-listening, his sense of knowing in advance what Jimi is saying, and not wanting to hear it, is an act of silence.

Is it a small world . . . ?
Not until lately.
. . . or what?
That's my question.

"You'll have to tell me about restaurants, health clubs, all the coolest stuff to do. Oh, and a card game? What's the best night? Hey, we could even double-date. Did we ever do *that* in the old days? Soon, homeboy."

The world is shrinking. It has become a small world. *Or what?*

He brings their lunch and his notebook to the living room and sits beside Hettie, who has fallen asleep.

Shrek sits alone under the light of the moon, in great pain, because he now believes that Princess Fiona—with whom he has fallen in love and who had seemed, at moments, to be falling in love with him as well—really thinks of him as an ugly ogre, which he is, not the gentle, affectionate, strong-willed, goodhearted, loyal man he also is and would in fact be, if she did reciprocate his feelings.

If *Shrek* had been written by Chekhov this is where it would end.

But that's the hardest irony to manufacture in a work of literature, and to accept in life: What we think we are, or fear we might be, is often, in fact, what we truly are, only more so.

On the top of a blank notebook page, he writes two entries from Chekhov's notebooks:

A pregnant woman with short arms and a long neck, like a kangaroo.

A man in conversation: "and all the rest of it."

Then adds:

A woman house painter, helpless and angry: I'm on the job seven days!

A man's voice on an answering machine: What a piss!

Is it a small world, or what?
A small world . . . ?
Or what?

A procession of thoughts arises faster than he can write them, but he tries to capture some portion of each one before it slips through the ragged gaps in his anxious, cluttered mind.

Great walls have been rising around us—we hadn't seen them clearly until the war started and they began to move closer and closer to each other—all of us contained within them will encounter each other more and more often.

A woman he's never seen before, now twice? A man he hasn't seen in more than thirty years.

Why do we find reoccurrence and coincidence surprising? Because we usually encounter most things and most other living creatures—outside family, friends and proximate daily stuff—only once? Or what?
Except in books and movies.

On each morning since the war started, our history has narrated itself from within an increasingly shrinking country.

Molecules trapped in contracting space bounce off the walls that confine them, accelerate their movements, and collide with increasing frequency.

Lois Lane and Jimmy Olsen are thrown into a cell by gangsters. An arm pulls down a lever, and the two opposing side walls begin to move toward each other. They shout for help. Jimmy tries to stop the walls' advance by pushing against them, first one, then the other. Then they both begin running back and forth in the diminishing space. Where's Superman? They stand beside each other, hold hands, wait sadly, calmly, for what they cannot prevent.
But then Lois tells Jimmy, "We have only one chance," and as she says this, the walls stop where they are, just far enough apart for Lois and Jimmy to stand beside each other, facing forward.
We know that the walls will remain in this position only briefly.

Once Lois has finished saying what she has to say, and once Jimmy has responded, they will continue moving toward each other like the sides of a vise, until they complete their steady and total eradication of space.

"We can become new creatures."

Jimmy, barely more than a teenager, his camera still slung around his neck, is too frightened to even tell her he cannot understand.

"We can allow our bodies to lose their substance. We can become people made solely of color and light."

Jimmy looks at the wall pressed against him, looks forward again, begins to shiver and weep. "We can do that?"

Lois puts an arm around his shoulder. "Of course we can, Jimmy. You and me. We'd be like Shrek and Princess Fiona."

9

Tom wakes on the couch, with Hettie sitting on his lap, pressing the top of her head against the underside of his chin. Outside the windows it's dark. Joan is standing between them and the TV, which is still on, pointing the camera at them.

"You're awake?" she says. "A second ago you opened your eyes but didn't wake up. Wait," she says, sets the camera on the coffee table, sneezes, then picks it up again. "I keep thinking this cold has gone away, then it comes back."

Half of Hettie's sandwich has been eaten and a bite has been taken out of his. He hears the voice of a newscaster from the cable news station, which was the last channel he and Joan had watched yesterday and which must have come on after *Shrek* ended. Joan is still wearing her coat.

"If you're awake, you can smile."

Joan depresses the button on the top of the camera but nothing happens. She holds the camera away from herself and examines it. "We didn't finish this roll. Or have we?" She opens the back of the camera, takes out a finished roll of film then sets the camera on the coffee table, walks into the kitchen and comes back with a new roll of film. She picks up the camera by the wrist lanyard and, with a look of surprise says, "Hey, this thing, the cord, it's all wet." She looks at Hettie, now sitting on the other end of the couch, then at him. They're both staring into the TV screen.

She steps in front of the TV again, this time deliberately, so they have to look at her, then aims the lens at them and motions with her hand for them to move together. Hettie stays put so Tom moves to her side. Joan takes a picture. Then she sits on the couch with Hettie and he takes one.

"Hey, this is wet," he says, holding the lanyard away from the camera itself.

"I just told you that," Joan says. "Do you know how this got wet?" she asks Hettie.

Hettie reaches for the camera now, and he hands it to her. She raises it to her eye and takes a picture of the TV screen.

"You know how to use that?" Joan asks her. "At three?"

Hettie takes another picture of the TV.

"She's a genius," he says.

Joan reaches her hand toward Hettie, who reluctantly hands her the camera. "You sure you don't know how this got wet?" she asks once more before leaving the room.

When she returns she has a plate of sliced pears, the apartment prospectus Hettie had left on the kitchen table, and a credit card bill, which she hands to him after setting down the plate. "This came yesterday. Would you call them this month? I'm tired of these people. Each time it's someone else, and each time it's like I'm talking to a mountain goat."

Without their knowing it, at a point in time at least six months ago, they paid their credit card bill without knowing that somewhere on it was a box they were supposed to check that said, *No, we don't want credit-card theft insurance.* Each month's bill since has included an additional eight-dollar charge for the insurance they neither asked for nor knew they were supposed to decline. On each of those months Joan has called them, had the charge removed, and been told that it would no longer appear on their bill.

"I wonder how much money they've made from people who don't watch each bill to see whose hands are slipping into their pockets," she says.

Then she holds up the prospectus.

"Your daughter brought that home," Tom tells her.

Joan sits on the couch between them and asks Hettie if she's ready to move out on her own. Hettie, her eyes glued to the TV, doesn't answer, so his wife picks up the remote, and presses the mute button. She then reads the prices of the apartments aloud, and says to Hettie, who still hasn't taken her eyes from the screen, "If you move to this place your neighbors might be the folks that sent us this credit card bill."

On the TV is the still image of a young soldier, sitting behind a machine gun atop an armored vehicle. An endless reach of darkness surrounds the brightly lit area he occupies. His night vision goggles are flipped up over the front of his helmet.

"A high school friend we ran into on the way home might be another of our new neighbors."

"Who?"

"Jimi DelVecchio. Haven't seen him since 1970. We ran into him on the way home, along with a bunch of other folks waiting to see the condos." He points to the prospectus she's still holding.

When he turns back to the TV a horizontal line splits the screen in half. On the bottom a man repeatedly hits golf balls off a tee with a comically awkward swing: one lands in a swimming pool in a suburban back yard beside a family sitting at a picnic table, one bounces off the top of a city bus, another lands in a garbage can. On the top another man hits just one golf ball, in a slow, graceful swing that sails in slow motion through a long arc before landing on a green, then rolling in a straight line toward the hole in which it falls just before the image disappears and the entire screen is occupied by an attractive couple driving an SUV that zooms into the distance, disappears over a rise, then reappears from the front as it pulls up to the entrance of a rustic country inn.

"You know him well?"

"I think I once did. Now I don't know him at all. People can change as much within a single lifetime as they can between one life and another."

"The Buddha said that?"

"All I can say about the new, state-of-the-art Jimi is that he'd probably watch the commercials on this news station with serious attention, consider the products and services they sell, and judge them to be, along with the news stories they punctuate, viable representations of the world as he knows it."

The image of the soldier atop the armored vehicle returns to the screen, and a reporter standing beside him is reaching a microphone up to him so he can speak into it. Tom asks his wife, who is closer to the remote, to turn on the sound. The reporter interviewing the soldier asks him what he expects when they reach Baghdad.

"We're gonna give em a beatin," the soldier says.

"She shouldn't be hearing this," Joan says, and reaches again for the remote.

"Just let him finish," Tom says.

"Do you expect to encounter much resistance?" the reporter asks.

"There could be," the soldier says, and then points upward. "But before we get there we'll send some serious messages from the sky."

Joan turns the TV off, pulls Hettie onto her lap, and says, "Don Quixote went crazy from reading too much. He slipped into a world made of words—and never returned."

Something she has said makes Hettie laugh.

"He didn't want to," Tom says. "That's crazy and not crazy."

"I think the scale tilts more to the crazy side. I bet something like that can happen if you watch news channels too much."

"I keep watching to find something in the background," Tom says, "something at the edge of the story that tells me what's really happening." He points toward the edge of the darkened TV screen. Hettie looks at the spot he points to. "But we never really get it— we never really get it. If you lose it from watching too much news, you don't climb onto an old horse, put on a hand-made helmet, and set off on a mission no one but you understands. One day you discover that, in increments, the way animals adapt in small stages to changes in their environment, you've been recognizing yourself in the commercials between the stories. The world has been reduced in size to something unforeseeably simple and addictive—the narrow path between what you have and what you'd like to have."

"It could be a new strain of Stockholm Syndrome," Joan says, "that slowly makes you forget who you were before you had it. You might even believe you're happy."

Hettie starts laughing again and this time stands up on her mother's lap, bounces, and then falls back to a sitting position.

"She hears the word 'happy,'" Joan says, "and she becomes happy."

Tom kisses the top of Hettie's head and says, "You're the only one in the room who's not crazy."

Comedy

March 25

But as time & experience do reforme every thing that is amisse, so this bitter poeme called the old Comedy, *being disused and taken away, the new* Comedy *came into place, more civill and pleasant a great deale and not touching any man by name . . .*
—George Puttenham, *The Arte of English Poesie*, 1589

I heard that the military was developing robot soldiers. I heard Gordon Johnson of the Joint Forces Command at the Pentagon say: "They don't get hungry. They're not afraid. They don't forget their orders. They don't care if the guy next to them has just been shot. . . . "
—Eliot Weinberger, *What I Heard About Iraq*

10

Of the children old enough to follow the condensed version of *A Midsummer Night's Dream* being performed at Violet's school, those who were still watching at the point when Bottom, whose head had been transformed into the head of a donkey, awakes to find his human face restored, were sorely disappointed. When the boy playing him sat up, yawned, and rose to his feet without the huge, fur-covered ears and papier-mâché snout, even before he touched his face and said, "Methought I was, and methought I had . . . ," they began booing and shouting. Because of all the noise, several of the younger children started to cry. Then some of the older boys began making fart sounds by blowing against their hands. From then on, as far as the children were concerned, it was all over. The performance continued nevertheless.

They are now in the last act: the wedding of Theseus, a smiling boy waving regally to the audience, and Hippolyta, played by a bored, distracted Violet. Only the adults, many of them laughing or trying with difficulty not to, are still watching.

Tom is in the front row of the audience, made up of parents, children and teachers, sitting on the floor of the school's cafeteria. Even with the clamor, Hettie, nested in his crisscrossed legs, leaning back against his chest, has remained asleep.

He pulls out his notebook and a pen from his coat pocket and begins to write down a thought he just had. He writes a quick, sloppy, run-on sentence in the hope of getting it all down before the play ends or Hettie wakes up:

In the consciousness of children there resides an ancient and more absolute comprehension of destiny formed during the countless millennia before life offered the necessary conditions for the invention of comedy (the idea of choice, and the possibility that what is unexpected might not always be dangerous), a period when childhood and adult life occurred as a single continuous arc, uninterrupted by stations or second chances, that began the moment we could walk and feed ourselves, had accrued enough of a past to have, in some form, memory and some notion of a future, and ended decades or weeks later, with death: if along the way you change into something, as a tadpole becomes a frog, or a man a donkey, your fate, with no exceptions, is to remain the thing you changed into.

❁

As he writes the last of these words, the woman sitting next to them asks him what he is writing. When he turns to her she says, "Are you a reporter embedded in P.S. 90?"

Just then Puck, a wreath of plastic leaves encircling his head, standing alone in the stage area, says, "Give me your hands, if we be friends . . . " then shouts, "That means clap," and before he finishes his one last line the audience is applauding, shouting, and whistling. Hettie wakes and begins clapping, too, as if she'd already been doing so in her dream.

"It's just a thought I had," he tells her, "about the play. Something I didn't want to forget."

"What's the thought?" she says. "If you don't mind my asking."

The applause quickly thins out and then slows to a stop. Hettie becomes restless in the silence that follows, as if just now realizing that she's woken up, and begins to rock back and forth against his chest.

The woman slides closer to them, leans forward and smiles at Hettie, then lightly touches her cheek.

Hettie stops rocking, but rather than acknowledging the woman, she looks up at him.

"It was about the kids' response to Bottom getting his own face back," he says. "Children can be kind of absolute. If you change, they sometimes want you to stay the thing you changed into."

"I think they just liked him better that way," the woman says, then introduces herself. "Victoria." She takes his hand, then reaches for Hettie's hand, which she shyly allows her to take.

This time Hettie looks back at her and immediately roots her eyes on her cleavage, and the two tattoos, rainbow-colored strands of entwined vines that arch over her breasts before disappearing below the neckline of her black sweater.

❖

Tom and Hettie were the first members of the audience to arrive. He wanted to make sure they got a seat in the front where Violet could see them. After signing in with the police officer sitting behind a desk just inside the front door, they walked across the wide hall, then through the double doors that led into this enormous room, in which two maintenance workers were sliding the long lunch tables across the floor, one pushing one pulling, and lining them up against the wall. When the tables were all cleared away and the men had left, he and Hettie, holding hands, stood in the center of the huge, empty, weirdly peaceful room. The floor they stood on, and that surrounded them—an enormous expanse of concrete painted a smooth dark red—was gently hilled and valleyed like a calm sea. They did not speak.

After five minutes a woman came in and set stacks of serving bowls, napkins, and juice boxes on the outermost of the tables that had been dragged to the side of the room. She then left and, a moment later, returned. This time she introduced herself as Judith, the principal, and asked if he and Hettie could help her lay a long strip of silver gaffing tape across a stretch of floor near the front of the room. He held the roll while the woman unreeled the tape. Once Hettie understood what they were doing, she happily helped him hold one end, move it slightly this way, slightly that way until it was just right, then, scrunched down and sidestepping, pressed it firmly to the floor. After Judith left a second time they sat down right behind the tape facing the center of what they assumed would be the stage.

After five more long minutes they heard the sound of footsteps. Though they were muffled by the carpet of paint, the echoes bouncing off the walls of the large empty room grew louder and seemed to multiply: they turned, expecting to see a number of people, but saw only one, the woman who would later introduce herself as Victoria, halfway between where they sat and the double doors they'd entered earlier, walking in their direction.

"Where is everyone?" she asked, then dropped her shoulder bag and sat down beside them. She took out her cell phone and opened it. "Ten, no, eight minutes till show time."

A group of adults and younger children, who seemed to have arrived together, were now coming into the room and seating themselves on the floor behind them.

Then her cell phone, which she had placed beside her, emitted a quick, musical ring that he thought might be a sped up version of "Lara's Theme" from *Dr. Zhivago*. "Time to turn this off," she said.

※

"Do you know anyone in the play?" Victoria now asks Hettie, as they watch Judith arrange the actors on "stage" to have their picture taken.

He can see that Hettie likes her. Victoria is plump and buxom and sexy; she doesn't change her tone of voice when she speaks to Hettie, and doesn't hesitate before touching her cheek or tucking a stray hair behind her ear.

"We're here to see Violet," Tom says, looking down at Hettie, whose eyes are once again riveted to the tattoos.

"You her uncle or something?" Victoria asks him. "Is Violet your cousin?" she asks Hettie.

"We're her neighbors," he says. "We're friends of Hannie and Jolie and Violet."

Victoria notices the direction of Hettie's stare and points to one of the tattoos, giving him permission to look as well. "Crowns of thorns without the thorns," she says. "The tattoo artist did them from a drawing I made."

"You're an artist?" he asks.

"Textile designer. I design clothes, too. In fact, I designed these." She points to her gray Capri pants covered with a pattern, in black lines, of 1950s-ish teenage girls with ponytails, talking on telephones that are all connected by a single squiggly wire. "This design was on a lunchbox my mother had when she was Violet's age. She kept it even after she grew up. Then I used it, too, when I went to school. She takes Hettie's finger, points it at one of the ponytailed girls on her leg. "I bet you want your own phone. Am I right?"

Hettie looks at him, considering the question, gauging his response, too, then nods, yes.

"Who are you here to see?" he asks Victoria.

"Who . . . ?"

"Do you have a kid in the play?"

"Oh, yeah. Jess. My partner's son. He plays the little boy who comes to live with the fairies."

"The changeling boy," he says.

"Yeah, but don't tell him that. He thinks it means a kid who still wears diapers."

He and Victoria are standing in the same area where they'd been sitting during the play. Violet, Jess, and Hettie sit beside them on the floor. Jess, who at seven had been the youngest student in the play, keeps walking back to the snack table and then returning with handfuls of grapes and potato chips and Pirate Booty for Hettie and Violet, who is still wearing red rouge and a silver gown made from a spray-painted adult-size T-shirt. Her bright green fairy hair is covered by the gold cardboard crown she wore, as Hippolyta, in the final scene.

He tells Violet that in the original, grownup version of the play, the whole story might be Hippolyta's dream. Instead of responding to what he says, she takes off the crown and places it on Hettie's head. It slips down over her eyes and face, but Violet lifts it back up and adjusts it. Hettie looks back at her, unsmiling and thoughtful, attempting to understand the identity it adds to hers. After a moment they both laugh.

"The story was Hippolyta's dream?" Victoria asks him. "How?"

"You could read it that way. In this version she doesn't show up until the end, but in the original we learn, in the first scene, that Theseus *wooed her with his sword*. I think that's how he put it. She was the queen of the Amazons and, after his army conquered them, he brought her back to Athens, against her will, to become his bride."

"She seems so happy in the play."

"At the end she does. The dream she has, with all the who-loves-who business is her coming to terms with her fate. She had no choice. She had to marry Theseus."

"*That's* an old story, isn't it?" she says, nodding to solidify what she seems certain is their shared agreement.

He points to Jess. "Even the changeling boy. He was kidnapped like Hippolyta—snatched from the world of mortals, and brought to the land of the fairies."

"He seems happy, too," she says, then adds, "But wait. The other characters are real. At least they *seem* real. The stuff that goes on actually happens to them, no?"

"That's often the way things work in classical drama. They are, on one hand, people carried away by the romantic silliness of a midsummer night, and on the other hand they are citizens whose fate it is to live out the dreams of the royal house."

"Shit," she says, then looks at the children to see if they can hear. "Shit, shit, shit. That's what's going on *now*. With this fucking war." Her eyes follow Jess, who walks back over to the snack table and returns carrying three juice boxes with pictures of Grover from *Sesame Street* on them. When she turns back there are tears streaming down her cheeks.

Tom waits for her to speak but she doesn't. She takes one of the juice boxes, removes the straw attached to the side, pokes it into the top, and hands it to Hettie.

"Are you okay?" he asks her.

"My brother," she says. "He's in the army reserves. And they're shipping him over there. Maybe next week."

"I'm sorry," he says. "I hope the worst of it is over by then."

"For years Jamie's been living the royal-house dream—is that what you called it?—though if you just watched him living his life day by day, you wouldn't know it. You'd think he had a million choices, and made all his own stupid decisions, just like the people in the play."

Jess, seeing that she's upset, hands her his juice box. She takes a sip and hands it back. "You are so sweet," she says to him. She sits down now, beside the children, and he sits beside her.

"He's ten years younger than me. Only twenty-four but he already has a daughter older than Jess. He lives in Indiana. That's where we come from—a small town right in the middle of the state."

Jess turns at the mention of his name, but quickly returns to their game. He and Violet are handing bits of Pirate Booty to Hettie, who either eats them herself or places the crunchy ball in one of their mouths.

"I might as well tell you. That is, if you want to hear all this."

"The kids are very happy, sitting here."

"When Jamie was a junior in high school his girlfriend, Tabatha, got pregnant. Where I come from, what they can do to teenagers is a crime. You grew up here?" she asks Tom, and he nods. "It's not easy to explain to someone from New York. Living here I can barely understand it myself. It's not just religion or Rush Limbaugh or stuff like that. That's just what it looks like from here. It's like if you walk up to a bunch of teenagers waiting on line to get into a movie, you'll hear the shouts of the people they keep swallowed deep inside. I know that's dramatic and doesn't make sense. At first what you'll notice is a crowd of teenagers dressed like adults—for people that young, it's like they're imitating trees that have lost their leaves. Then you think you've just wandered into something unlikely and weird, like an anti-beauty contest."

He smiles then laughs, though he tries not to.

She laughs a bit, too. "It is a funny thing to say. I got out of there fifteen years ago, just after my mother passed away. Talking like that, making everything funny, is talking like the New Yorker I've become. Anyway, in the middle of that environment, nobody would consider letting them get an abortion. Not my father, not the born-again idiot he married six months after my mother died. I don't think Tabby or Jamie could even use the word. So Tabby quit school. After Hazel was born—she was named for my mother—they lived with her parents. Jamie found a night job cleaning department stores in the Tippecanoe Mall so that he could finish high school. He wanted to go to Purdue and study computer engineering, but that never happened. They couldn't stand living with her parents so they moved into their own apartment, but for that the night job wasn't enough. He found day jobs—seasonal farm work, janitor, lift operator in a scrap metal yard. Even with the day jobs he never earned enough, so he joined the reserves. The life he's been living? The life he lives now? He couldn't have dreamed that up. Somebody nasty did that for him." She begins to weep. "Or to him."

She rises to her feet again. He stands up as well, understanding that she doesn't want to remain at eye level with the children.

She looks around the room, and he follows her gaze. Perhaps half the audience has now gone. Speaking slowly, sadly, she says, "We no longer believe that things are what they appear to be. Not since the war started, not in a long time. It affects the way we think about everything. I mean, why can't it be that these kids simply like Bottom better as a donkey?"

Before he can answer, Victoria says, "You ever wonder why a pizza cutter never cuts through the bottom of a take-out box?"

"What?"

"I'm serious. You're never curious about that?"

Tom would laugh, now, if her eyes weren't still filled with tears.

"I mean, how come it's sharp enough to leave all those scratches in those big, round pie trays, but never cuts through such a thin layer of cardboard?"

He shakes his head.

"I always wondered about that. So last week I decided to go to the source. I asked this guy Mike, who works in the pizza place on my corner, and you know what he said? He said when you cut it in the box you don't press as hard."

"Wow," he says, smiling now.

"And now I'm wondering if maybe years ago, before I started worrying about what things appeared to be as opposed to what they were, before every word was part of a TV commercial . . . I'm wondering if back then the answer to a simple question like that might have occurred to me before I asked it."

After saying this she begins to weep again. "Shit," she says, then leans toward him so he can hug her.

He hadn't realized, till that moment, how much taller than him she is. And when she steps back he says, "You're really tall."

She laughs when he says that and then the kids stand up so they can all compare their own heights with hers and his and each other. They all start laughing when she stands on her toes and shows them how she can rest her chin on the top of Tom's head.

11

Hannie opens her door with the loosening smile and wet eyes of someone just finishing a long bout of hearty laughter.

Violet slips in past her, leading Hettie by the hand, and the two walk through the kitchen and into the next room of the floor-through apartment, a replica of their own, where Jolie, who is sitting in her bouncy-chair, is going whoop, whoop, whoop, whoop. They stand beside her facing a TV, which he can hear but not see from where he is standing.

"Come in," Hannie says, beginning to laugh again, and leads him into the room.

On the screen the Three Stooges are chasing each other around a couch where a plump, matronly woman is primly sitting. She turns her head as each of them circles past, bewildered at their behavior. None of the Stooges ever catches the one ahead, but with each circuit their pace increases, and as her head swings back and forth, faster and faster, her marcelled hair becomes more and more disheveled. She's wearing a string of large pearls around her neck, as well as a lorgnette, which hangs down to her bosom.

Violet and Hettie watch silently, with no expression on their faces. Jolie continues repeating whoop, whoop, whoop, whoop. . . .

"Wait," Hannie says. She picks up the remote and rewinds the tape: the Three Stooges circle the couch, in reverse direction, at high speed; Larry and Curly leave the room backward; Moe, kneeling on one foot before the woman, watches them leave; Moe awkwardly rises to his feet; the three of them are now in another room, the heel of Moe's fist rises suddenly above Larry's head, windmills around backwards, and stops in front of him where it meets the palm of his other hand; Larry backs away; Curly skips toward Moe, moving his hands in front of him. Hannie stops the tape, plays it forward again. Now Curly makes his hilarious horse-galloping sound: a quick cycle of finger snaps on both hands, followed by the slap of the flat of one hand against the top of the fist of the other.

While he does this repeatedly, he stares at Moe, does a zany foot-chopping back step and chants whoop, whoop, whoop, whoop.

Violet imitates the step and sound and gets it right the first time. She then stops and looks back at everyone. They're all laughing now. Then Hannie does it, too, and Violet starts up again, and he picks up Hettie and does the back step and now all five of them are going whoop, whoop, whoop, whoop.

He and Hannie leave the children in front of the TV and go back to the kitchen. She takes two beers from the refrigerator, unscrews the tops of them both, and sets one in front of him. She sits, reaches the bottle she is holding over to his side of the table, taps it against his, and says, "Cheers," sips, and says, "So how was the play?" but then quickly says, "Shit," leans over and slides the beer she'd just set in front of him over to her side of the table. "Tom, I'm sorry. I forgot."

"Don't worry," he says.

She opens the refrigerator door, looks inside, and says, "Orange juice, apple juice, Diet Pepsi with no caffeine."

"Pepsi," he says. "The play was terrific. Violet was great. The audience loved the performance but at one point criticized the playwright. Most of the children felt that once Bottom had been changed into a donkey he should have stayed that way. How was *your* day?"

"Good. And *easy*. I can't believe it. I actually feel relieved." She places a two-liter bottle of Diet Pepsi in front of him, sits, and sips her beer. "I want to keep that feeling as long as I can." She looks at the bottle for a moment, stands again, takes a glass from the drain board and sets it next to the Diet Pepsi.

"Tell me more," he says.

"I was expecting a day from hell. First thing, when we got there, I unpacked all the stuff from home—photographs, chotchkies, the two coffee mugs with the girls' handprints on them, her bedside lamp, stuff like that, and laid them around the room where she could see them. After I got her comfortable I tried to get her to eat some lunch, but she wouldn't even open her mouth, so I sat down on the bed and the two of us spent like forty minutes staring at the tray with her soup and pudding and protein shake. We would have stayed like that all afternoon if this wonderful young aide named John hadn't strolled in and said to her, 'Sarah, dear, let's go to the movies.' She looked at him like he was crazy, and like maybe she was angry, too, but then she smiled, sort of, which was all he needed. All I needed, too. Before she even realized what was happening, he picked her up from the bed and settled her in this big comfy recliner, reorganized her IV stand and oxygen, walked out of the room, then walked back in with two videotapes and a Dixie Cup of vanilla ice cream and one of those little flat wooden spoons wrapped in paper. He popped the first tape into the VCR—The Marx Brothers, *Coconuts*—and proceeded to feed her the ice cream, which she let him do. I think she understood everything that was going on. She hasn't been that alert, that present, in weeks. We just sat there and watched. She actually *laughed*. At least twice.

"John came and went but was there, with us, more than he wasn't, and when the movie was over he immediately popped in the second one. As the credits were rolling he said to my mother, 'Sarah, do you know this one? *The Apartment*? It's my all-time favorite.' He then warned her that he always cries at the end when Shirley MacLaine tells Jack Lemmon, 'Shut up and deal.'" She sips her beer. "I'd never seen it before. It's also got that guy who played the father in *My Three Sons*."

"Fred MacMurray."

"That's his name? He didn't have his pipe in this one. Anyway, me and John *both* cried at the end, and when I looked over at my mother I saw that she'd fallen asleep. So that's what we did all afternoon. Watch movies."

"Sounds wonderful."

"And when I was leaving John asked me what other movies I thought she might like to see, and what movies *I* might like to see, too, and I remembered how much she liked the Three Stooges. We used to watch them together when I came home from school. He said he didn't think they had them in their library but I could bring any videos I wanted to, so I stopped into Kim's Video on the way home. I was going to rent them but, by coincidence, they had the Three Stooges on sale. Seven ninety-five for six episodes."

She gets up, goes inside, and when she comes back she has Jolie in her arms. "You hungry?" she asks her daughter, who looks at him, then starts to fidget and cry. Hannie brings her back into the room where his daughter and Violet are still watching the Three Stooges. As Hannie sets her back in her bouncy chair and closes the Velcro belt, Violet claps and shouts, "Yay," to celebrate Jolie's return. Then Hettie claps and shouts, too.

"The Three Stooges have been reunited," Hannie says, when she returns to the table.

"I don't want to break up the act," he tells her, "but we should get going soon."

"Have *you* ever seen *The Apartment*?" she asks.

"I have. It's a terrific movie."

"Do you remember the part where Shirley MacLaine tries to commit suicide?"

"Uh huh."

"I'm just thinking now. I'm sitting in this place where people wait to die . . ."—she stops here, and shudders—"In this place, beside my mother, who was awake at this point or not awake, I don't know, and we're watching this woman trying to kill herself, trying to make herself *be* dead, and nobody gave it a thought."

"Sounds like a good thing," he says, "that you could both take a break from the whole idea."

"Like being in the eye of the storm. I want to stay there." She leans her head toward the other room. "And you should stay, too. At least finish your Diet Pepsi. The girls are fine."

"Do you know Victoria?" he asks.

"Jess's mom's partner?"

He nods.

"She doesn't own a thing with a high neckline." She points to her chest, moves her finger in the shapes of Victoria's tattoos. "On the days she picks up Jess every kid in the classroom is staring right here."

"A crown of thorns without the thorns."

"You might be the first person she told. I've been wondering if they go all the way around. Did you ask?"

"I wanted to."

"Usually Melanie, Jess's other mom, picks him up, so I don't really know much about Victoria—except that she talks too much. Lately, when I see her, I keep my distance. She usually goes on and on about her mother. I don't have time for that right now."

"Her brother's in the reserves. He's shipping out to Iraq soon."

"Oh shit," Hannie says and shakes her head. She downs the rest of her beer, lifts the one she'd opened for him and takes a sip, then gets up, walks inside, and stands facing the TV.

12

When Tom and Hettie get home, Joan, sitting at the kitchen table, says, "Guess who I just had a talk with?" The handset of the cordless phone sits on the table in front of her, beside an unopened delivery bag from the Bamboo Pavilion restaurant with a folded menu stapled across its closed top.

"I'll give you a hint. 'I'm a *blast* from your husband's *past*.'"

"Jimi? What did he want?"

"I wish you'd gotten home earlier, when you were supposed to"—she points to the grease splotches sprouting on the sides of the brown paper bag—"you could've asked him that yourself." Her face tightens into a pre-sneeze frown. She inhales suddenly, raises a balled-up clump of paper towel to her face, but the sneeze doesn't come. "I don't know if this is a new cold or if it's still the last one."

Hettie laughs, tries to skip backwards, and shouts "whoop, whoop, whoop, whoop," then runs over to Joan for a hug and climbs onto her lap.

"She watched the Three Stooges at Hannie's," he says.

She kisses the top of Hettie's head, then sneezes. "Jimi wanted your email address. I sneezed before, too, when I was talking to him, right into the phone, and you know what he said? He said, 'I want you to know, good woman, that your misery has company. My wife caught every single cold the kids brought home from school.' Then he asked if I would talk to her."

"His wife? About what?"

"New York. She's afraid of it and always has been. And now that the idea of moving here has become a reality, she has—in his words—gone off the deep end. Two nights ago she had a dream that because of the war there'd soon be another terrorist attack. It would be here, in New York, and a lot worse than the first one. She wants to stay in the Washington suburb where they live, pull their son out of Columbia before he even starts, and send him to a college someplace else."

"What does he want you to tell her?"

"How safe it is. How we like raising our daughter here. And all the good stuff like Broadway musicals and museums and restaurants and shopping. Just by being your wife, I'm the friend of *his* wife."

"You told him you'd do this?"

She points to her chest. "June Cleaver: housewife, mother, Homeland Security agent."

Hettie squirms on her lap, smiles, holds her eyes fixed to the spot Joan had pointed to on her chest.

Joan unbuttons the top buttons of her blouse, barely conscious of doing so, and lifts the cup of her brassiere, but Hettie, who still occasionally nurses, doesn't want to. Instead, she says, "Tattoos around *your* nanas?"

"What's that about?" she asks him.

He tells her about the play, about Victoria, and about Hannie's day at the hospice.

Hettie again says, as a question, "Tattoos around your nanas?"

"Honey," Joan says, "would you like me to get a tattoo?"

"I would," Tom says.

❖

Tom is sitting on the couch, reading the revision of Nick's story, now titled "The Plumber's Divorce." Joan walks in and sets a photo envelope from Rite-Aid on the coffee table.

"She's asleep," she says, then turns on the news, mutes the sound and watches, with the hearing-impaired captions stretching across the screen beneath the word crawl.

"Now that I think of it," she says, "it's not impossible that since October I have had one single, endless fucking cold. Just when I think it's gone it washes over me again like a giant wave."

On the screen a family with four children and a basset hound rush out the front door of their house in comically sped-up motion and unload, from the SUV parked in the driveway, a kayak, a paddle, several pairs of skis, a full golf bag, a steamer trunk with stickers all over the sides, a trombone, an antique lamp, and a double dog bowl with the name *Buster* printed on its side. Then—still at high speed—the father pulls up the seats in the back, he, his wife, the children and the dog get in, they back out of the driveway, and as they begin to move forward, the suburban street they are driving on is transformed into a tree-lined country road. At this point action slows to normal, the wife turns from the passenger seat to smile at her family, and the words "Everybody and Everything" appear as a caption across the bottom of the screen.

"I wish we had a car," Joan says.

He nods toward the photo envelope. "What's that?"

"I want to show you something when you're done reading."

He puts down the manuscript. He has read only the first page of "The Plumber's Divorce," which remains unchanged since the previous draft.

"I picked these up on my way home from school." She slips out the photos and sets them on her lap. She then lifts off the top half, like she is cutting a deck, and hands it to him. The top photo looks like a pale, quadrangular headlight seen through dense fog. "I already separated the doubles," she says, "so we can look at them at the same time. Like a slide show."

He peeks at the second and third in his stack. They are variations of the first.

"Wait for me," Joan says.

"What is this?" He holds the first one up.

"The finished roll of film I took out of the camera on Sunday." She points to the photo on the top of the stack. "Hettie went on a photo safari without our knowing about it. I believe the first few are the TV."

Following the images of the TV are six shots out the front window of the buildings across the street. Even with the halo reflection of the flash on the windowpane, he can still see the familiar flowerpots in two of the windows directly across from theirs. Between the first and last image in the series, a row of pigeons on the roof of the next building grows in number from five to seven.

"I think these," he says, "are pictures of the world she was waiting for you to come home from."

"You think so?" Joan looks through them again, studying each one. "I'm going to save these," she says, then reaches into her blouse, withdraws her hand and looks at the small amount of wetness on the tips of her fingers. "More often than not, she falls asleep without nana. Motherhood makes you such a fucking sap."

They go through the stack, one at a time. Some of the images contain the altered shapes of objects that seem familiar—perhaps because they know the things themselves must be somewhere in the apartment—but are too blurred to identify.

He holds up a photograph of the kitchen window taken from across the room. "She took these over time," he says. "Over a period of days."

"How do you know that?"

He points to one side of a hazy brown rounded surface that fills most of the space between the camera and the window. "That's the table. And on Sunday, the whole time she had the camera, I was sitting right there."

Joan turns to face the TV screen. He follows her gaze and sees Donald Rumsfeld standing at a podium. The words *Saddam Fedayeen* appear in the strip of hearing-impaired captions. Joan picks up the remote and turns on the sound.

It's footage of a press conference that occurred earlier that day. A reporter has asked Rumsfeld about the increase in deadly attacks against American troops by paramilitary groups.

The reporter, finishing the question, says: "A statement your office issued earlier suggests that these groups are more organized than previously thought."

"Firstly," Rumsfeld answers, "the majority of coalition troops encountered little resistance and, as you know, have begun gathering just outside Baghdad." He looks directly at the reporter. "It would be nice to imagine that we would have encountered no resistance." He smiles and then unsmiles. "These folks you speak of, we're reducing their numbers quite rapidly. From the latest reports we're getting, I'd classify them as a short-term problem." Before he has finished with the last statement, the image of Rumsfeld standing at the podium is replaced by the image of him standing at the same podium just over a week ago, on the morning the first ground troops crossed the border into Iraq.

"Jesus," he says. "It's edited like a fucking movie."

"Not a whole movie," Joan says. "Like the coming attractions for something that's already happened."

In the older footage, Rumsfeld, after stating what the president had told everyone earlier, that the war had started, was responding to a question about the uncertain results of the "decapitation attack." This was the first day on which the press seemed to replace questions regarding the reasons for going to war with questions about the efficacy with which it was being fought. Instead of responding to the specific question, Rumsfeld answered—speaking to the Iraqis as much as, if not more than, to Americans—by saying that the initial phase of the war was mild compared to what was to come: "What will follow will not be a repeat of any other conflict. It will be of a force and a scope and a scale beyond what we have seen before."

Joan anxiously looks around the top of the coffee table, and then at the cushions of the couch they're sitting on.

"It's still in your hand," he tells her, and she turns off the TV.

✸

An hour later, Joan is sleeping restlessly on the other side of the couch. He has read another two pages of Nick's manuscript and still not a single word has changed. He picks up the stack of photos and flips through the last few they hadn't looked at before. The last one is probably the clearest of them all, but he can't make out what it is. A shiny snowy-white oval, surrounded only by darkness, with a black snaky thing curled in the shape of an S on one side.

"I agree with your assessment of why the kids responded the way they did when Bottom got his human face back, but I don't think Victoria

understood your point. Of course kids are in touch with all kinds of deep, basic, substantial human stuff. Much more than adults are."

"Do you think that her saying maybe they just liked it better that way, was a more immediate way of saying what I was saying?"

Joan rolls halfway over in her sleep, extends her feet behind his back and disrupts the internal conversation he's been having with her. It's the kind of inside-job dialogue he used to be able to maintain for hours on nights when he stayed at home and drank alone. With heroin it had been difficult to hold a thought long enough to respond to it, but alcohol, social drug that it is, encourages conversation, even when you're the only one in the room. Those nights of solo drinking were what made him aware that he'd done it since he was a child, though not for so long, or to the exclusion of everything else, as he had while drinking. It usually happens at night and most often when he's tired. The conversation can take the form of doubting what he was sure of earlier, or becoming sure of what he doubted earlier, or doing both intermittently. It starts as a self-to-self communication that's more biochemical cinema than words. Then the words come and the conversation blooms into a continuous process of unanimous agreement, each response fitting into place above the last thing said like the hands of the Three Musketeers as they are placed one atop the other on the hilt of a sword to symbolize their solidarity pledge: "All for one and one for all."

"The whole story has to be Hippolyta's dream. What else makes sense?"

"There's dreaming within the dream, too. The only one who truly knows what's going on is Puck. He's the only one who's got the whole picture. He even knows there's an audience out there watching."

Joan draws her feet back under her, turns forward, sets them on the floor and sits up against the back of the couch. She looks at him sleepily, then sneezes, twice. "It's spring," she says. "For the past week the lights on the Empire State Building are Easter-green. Has anyone even noticed?" She then points to the photo he's still holding in his hand. "Have you figured out what that is?"

He shakes his head.

"Try."

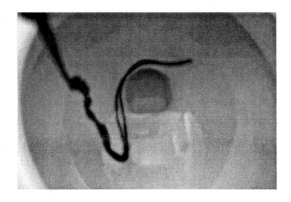

She smiles, picks up a copy of the same photo from her stack of doubles on the coffee table, and points to the snaky thing.

"I'm lost," he says.

"Remember the mystery of the wet camera lanyard?"

"The toilet?" he says.

Joan starts laughing and says, "I'm so proud of her." Her laughter turns into another series of sneezes. She stops, then changes the subject. "When you want to ask someone to do something like what Jimi asked me to do today, you're supposed to at least say something first, like, 'Would it be weird if I asked you a favor?' or 'I'll completely understand if you don't want to do this.' Instead he was like, 'Here's what I want you to do.'"

"I was thinking of that TV movie Hettie and I watched them shooting. In films and sitcoms it's funny when people talk too much about themselves to a cab driver or a bartender or someone sitting next to them on a plane."

"I suppose. But it's not at all funny when a living, breathing grown-up takes it for granted that a total stranger wants to hear all their shit. That's tragic—on both sides of the conversation."

"Speaking of comedy," he says, and then asks her, almost as if for the second time, if she thinks that seeing *A Midsummer Night's Dream* mainly as Hippolyta's dream is the way most people understand the play. "When I was a student, nobody talked about it that way."

"With this cold, even when I'm awake I feel like I'm dreaming."

13

Unable to sleep, Tom slides out of bed, goes into the living room, sits on the couch, picks up the revision of Nick's story, and this time reads it through to the end.

The revised narration doesn't begin until the main character, while driving home after feeding the PCP to her ex-husband's dogs, sees a wild dance of lights in her rearview mirror and then hears sirens approaching from a distance. At first she fears that her ex-husband has tipped off the police, or that possibly they'd been called by the woman whose toilet had been clogged, or that maybe it was a pack of drug dealers and crooked cops who'd gotten word that she was the one who'd taken the angel dust, probably worth thousands of dollars, and wanted it back. But then she sees a motorcycle gang member zoom past her, then another, and then a third with a very pregnant woman sitting on the front part of the seat, leaning backward against him. Then two motorcycle cops, followed by a squad car and an ambulance, speed past her.

The story also had a new ending. The following morning, when she is knocking on her neighbor's front door—she has come to tell him, Yes, she will go out to dinner with him—she notices the words, WOMAN IN LABOR, and just beneath them, FIRST RESPONDERS, in a bold headline on the folded newspaper lying on his doorstep. She is reading the paper when her neighbor, still in his bathrobe, opens the door.

The article is about a woman from out of town who had the bad luck to go into labor at the moment her car broke down. The woman called 911 on her cell phone, but before the police got there several members of the local chapter of the Hell's Angels passed by, circled around, and offered their help. Later, after a successful delivery, she told reporters that she would name her newborn daughter after the gang's leader, Vinnie.

Tom's not sure how happy he is with the new draft, but it's clear that Nick had listened and worked hard to revise it according to his suggestion—to add a more complex and personal sense of what it felt like for the plumber to experience the transition that is the result of the story's conflict.

He gets up, walks into the kitchen, returns with his notebook and a pen, but before he opens it he knows he has no wish to read anything he has written or to write anything new.

He turns off the light and stretches out on the couch. The room fills with an energized silence, the kind that fills a subway station after a train has pulled out and traveled beyond the point at which it can be heard, but leaves a dense swarm of molecules still dancing frantically in the air. Though he closes his eyes and lets his body settle into the cushions, he soon finds that he is panting and that his heart rate feels faster than it should. He can now feel the beats in one of his eyes and hears them when he covers his ears with his hands.

He presses the top pads of the fore- and middle fingers of his right hand against the pulse vein on his left wrist, holds them there until he gets a clear sense of the rhythm of the beats but doesn't start counting yet. He's waiting for the last of the luminous green numbers on the VCR's digital clock to change. It now reads 2:28. He will cross the entire minute that stretches between 2:29 and 2:30 counting the beats, but it takes several tries before he can count because he keeps confusing the rhythm of his own pulse with the meter of the colon throbbing between the hour and the minutes. He finally gains a steady hold on the count during the 2:34 minute, but before it has elapsed he hears his wife call him from the bedroom. He walks in and stands beside the bed.

"Can you turn it down?" she asks him.

"Turn what down?"

"Is it the TV? Turn it down."

"I'm not watching TV," he tells her. He listens for any sounds coming from the street or from their downstairs neighbor but hears none.

"Were you dreaming?" he asks, but she says nothing, because she is sound asleep.

He has sent her a message, but it was not delivered via the senses:

It moved through the same expanse of time, but in different space, as a pontoon travels a path separate from the boat it's attached to. The sound she heard was *inside* him.

❈

Back on the couch, he picks up his notebook, writes nothing in it.

❈

He turns on the TV with the sound muted. He channel surfs and stops at a movie in which a young man and woman in safari shorts and hats are walking toward the camera through a tunnel or cave. Because they are arguing—their body language and frustrated expressions imply they are a couple and have such arguments frequently—they do not notice the large boulder rolling at some distance behind them, picking up speed and beginning to catch up. She stops, angry at him, turns and takes a step in the direction they came from, sees the boulder, spins around again and runs quickly past him. He then looks behind himself, sees the boulder too—it is now very close—and runs just in front of it. Just before it overtakes him—he is now only a step or two behind her—she falls through a hole they didn't know was there, then he does. After falling a great distance—losing their hats on the way down—they land in some kind of underground lake. Treading water, they continue the argument where they left off.

Since he has been watching a silent TV he is surprised by a man's voice, loud and angry, rising from the street. "I can't even keep a pet . . ."

Tom walks back into the bedroom to see if the sound has reached Joan, who remains calmly asleep.

When he returns to the living room he hears a woman's voice from below, soothing and apologetic, loud enough to hear but not loud enough to pierce the glass of the closed window, as the man's voice had, with the words identifiably intact.

He walks to the window, looks down at the street. The man is standing on the sidewalk, a step in from the curb, leaning with one arm against a small tree, which bends slightly from his weight. The woman is standing in the street, a few feet away, facing him. "I can't keep anything. Nothing. Not a person, not even a . . ." The words he says become choked and indecipherable. Then he says, "Goddamn it."

They stop speaking. They stand this way for a long minute, then she steps toward him, up onto the sidewalk, reaches slowly into the side of his open jacket, and wraps her arm around him. He takes a step back, just out of her reach, crosses both arms against the tree, leans his head against them and begins to cry.

They are in that position when Tom returns to the couch, opens his notebook, and writes,

A man filled from his feet to his head with what has made him drunk. He is the vessel that contains it, and he is inside it, too, struggling to keep from drowning in everything he has ever lost.

❖

He then lays down the notebook, the pen holding the page he has just written on, and lies down, picks up the remote and with the sound still off turns back to the news.

❖

On the screen, is a pencil sketch of a courtroom scene: a robed judge sitting at the bench, followed by a cut to a suburban home with a strip of police tape stretched across the front of the house and another strip, enclosing a dug-up rectangular area, about as long and wide as a compact car, on its large front lawn.

Words and numbers sliding through the crawl beneath: "The Pentagon announced earlier that on the night of March 21st, the commencement of the aerial assault campaign known as Shock and Awe, more than 1500 precision weapons landed in the Iraqi cities of Baghdad, Tikrit, Mosul and Kirkuk."

Cut back to drawing of judge, now leaning toward two lawyers, a man and a woman, standing before bench. He is older, serious, with a look of paternal, ironic curiosity. His wide face above his wide neck emerging from the robe is likable and reassuring, like the wide front of a city bus.

Tom turns off the TV, writes two entries in his notebook.

A movie made entirely of comic relief—no tension, no suspense, no fear, no sadness, no tragic possibility to need relief from. The source of our need for this disburdening pause is tangled in the world outside the story: the knowledge that the leaders of our country have launched an attack of unprecedented ferocity against a country that has committed no act of aggression against them.

Sometime in the coming year Americans will see a made-for-TV movie or an episode of a situation comedy about adults in NYC who behave like self-involved children, in which a young woman who looks like, but may not be, Brooke Shields, will be complaining about the things in her life that cause her pain, though it will not seem like real pain, but trivial, childish, whimsically overstated pain that the audience will laugh at as they watch her expressing all of this to a man in a ridiculously oversized turban who barely understands English. And in that moment, moving quickly across the screen, there will appear some barely identifiable images of this tiny portion of the immeasurable world, the neighborhood where the scene has been shot and where he and his family live: a reflection of life so lacking in substance it could not cause the smallest flicker of a shadow on the wall of Plato's cave.

Tom hears the man's voice again from the street. He is crying loudly now, wailing like an animal.

By the time he reaches the window, the man has quieted down. He and the woman are now standing beside each other, their backs against the front of the building about ten feet in from the edge of the sidewalk where they were standing earlier. She sets one foot, then the other, six inches out in front of her, presses her hips and back against the wall, and then reaches her arm around his midsection. They are talking now, his voice louder than hers. Tom, across the street, four floors above, cannot understand enough of the words to know what they are saying to each other.

She appears drunk too, though not as helplessly drunk as him: She holds her arm firmly around him like a belt, bracing them both against the wall, as if the force of gravity will not hold them through the next rotation of the earth.

He knows so little about them. The rest of their story would have to be his.

He gets up off the couch, goes to his desk, turns on his computer, and checks his email. There's an unopened message from Jimi, sent at eleven p.m. As he stares at the screen, losing his gaze in the rows of dark letters hovering above the field of dull-bright color, a second new-message notification, in bolder print like the first one, appears silently on the screen. It's also from Jimi.

He goes off line without opening either of them and plays computer Solitaire, over and over, for close to half an hour and never wins a game. Then he returns to the couch and turns out the light.

He closes his eyes, wills the turbines in his chest to slow down and, as his body sinks into the cushions and a degree of stillness asserts itself, he sees a red jack slide across a luminous milk-white field and lay itself on top of a black queen.

14

Tom hears a whispering voice: *I want to tell you a story, but only if you promise not to write it down in your fucking notebook.*

Though it is made only of breath, like the skeleton of a flute's song, the voice is familiar.

We have met before, you and I, in a dream people were having while still awake.

Tom doubts he is asleep. He doubts he is awake.

Relax, you already know who I am. Puck then steps forward, emerging from the shaded crowd Tom talks to when he talks to himself, as if he's always been there. No longer whispering, now speaking in full voice—mischievous, childlike, demonic, feral—he says, *Just watch, and just listen. This isn't a story I'm telling solely for your benefit, it's a movie I'm broadcasting to an entire nation of dreamers. I'll call it*

A Dream to Wear Away This Long Age . . .

I begin by drawing your attention to the man sitting at the desk in the Oval Office. He is very tired. Can you see his heavy eyelids? Can you see his chin resting in his hands?

If in A Midsummer Night's Dream, *an imagined story of ancient times, it is the destiny of the young lovers and tradesmen, even that of the fairies of the night, to enact the dream in which Hippolyta—Queen of the Amazons, taken in battle by Theseus and brought to Athens to become his wife—undergoes the process of accepting her fate; if dreams dreamt in the royal house—sweet, melancholy, vexing or monstrous—become the fateful threads from which the hours and days of the citizenry are woven, then in a tale imagined in a democracy, would not the process be reversed? Would it not instead be the citizens themselves who have the dream? And then should not the players who find themselves enacting this dream be those who govern them?*

And so this man will undergo a transformation more radical in form than the one experienced by the business traveler who awoke to find he had become a beetle; more profound in substance than the moment the seer Tiresias reached down to discover that the body he'd known as a man's body was now that of a woman.

Watch him sit back in his chair. Watch him turn off his desk lamp and begin to rise slowly to his feet as the ceiling above him is replaced by the night's sky.

The next thing you will see is what he sees—a mysteriously luminescent stone wall, surrounded by darkness—and you will see it as he does, as if through an amber-colored lens.

"It's like looking through a glass of brandy," he says. If you can imagine that behind the mortar and stone is a source of light so powerful that a small portion of its radiance penetrates from the other side, you will see it as he does. Though he has not yet realized it, he's wearing a helmet and uniform, holding the stock of an M-16 tightly in his hands, and staring across the darkness at the wall.

He raises one hand from the trigger guard and, like Bottom touching what he expected to be his own face and finding, instead, the leathery snout of a donkey, he discovers the night-vision goggles and, above, the helmet.

"Am I myself and someone else?" he asks.

As if it were an answer to his question, we see an arm extend toward him from behind and a knuckle rap the back of his helmet. Conk, conk, conk.

We see a line of men, members of a patrol, standing behind him. The soldier closest to him raps his helmet again and says, "And now a message from the sky."

The body the president has found himself in instinctively knows what to do. It drops to the ground, faster, even, than gravity can pull it there.

At last he knows where he is.

My friends in the audience, place your hands over your ears.

What surprises him is not the enormity of the sound, but how the earth drops, then slams back up against his torso before he even hears it.

After the missile has struck, he remains there, holding his body to the ground, pressing his face into the dust.

"Will this ever end?" he asks, aloud, though does not know who he asks it of.

Look: See the faint lightening of the sky that tells us the top of the sun is about to show itself on the horizon.

Listen: Hear the voice of a muezzin intoning the call to prayer.

"Will this ever end?" he asks again, and here I add a question to his: What if, unlike Hippolyta, the dreamers will not accept their fate? Can this story end? Can the transformation ever be undone?

Now let your eyes adjust—not just because it's night once again, but because you're looking through the dimmed fluorescent light of a closed department store: There he is—this man who had been a president— wearing red coveralls and pushing a vacuum cleaner over an expanse of carpeted floor. Watch how he moves it through a maze of circular clothing racks with the slow, dexterous grace of someone who's been working at this job for a long time.

Unlike many who found themselves in this dream, he has survived. Yet in doing so, he did not return to the life he had lived before, but took the first steps along a different path, one that had its origin in his unexpected transformation. That path, over months and years, has brought him here.

Look beyond him. Can you see the person, also wearing red coveralls, walking toward him from the far side of the enormous store?

Although he does not see her, we do, and as she gets nearer we recognize her.

She calls his name as she approaches, though neither we, nor the man who had been a president, can hear a thing. Even if he could, he rarely turns his head when called by the name over the breast pocket of his coveralls. The recurring images from his first life reach him less and less often, and by this point in the dream, a mixture of fear, subdued restlessness, and exhaustion from work has become the largest part of who he knows himself to be.

Standing right in front of him now, she presses her thumb and forefinger together, twists her hand, and mouths, *Turn off the vac.* Over one pocket of her coveralls is her name; *Victoria,* over the other is the word *Supervisor.*

He turns off the vacuum cleaner and, instead of facing her, runs his eyes along the electric wire leading into it, as if looking backward through time, and finds the place where it disappears into the shadows.

"I've just come to say good-bye," Victoria tells him.

He looks back at her.

"I grew up in this town," she says, "but it's time to leave. You know I've only stayed around for my mother. Now that she's gone, I'm in the wind." She smiles, lowers herself to the floor, sits with her legs folded in front of her, and pats the floor for him to sit beside her.

He sits just where he'd been standing, a few feet away, facing her.

"Since this is my last night of work, I'm going to tell you something I've always wanted to tell you . . . if you want to listen, that is."

He nods, though otherwise his expression is blank.

"You know I like you, right?" Victoria says.

He nods again.

"Please remember that, even if what I'm going to say sounds weird. Okay?" She smiles, then says, "Okay, here I go. I sense there's a lot more to you than meets the eye, but in your case, frankly, there's very little for the eye to meet with."

He listens, hears, and understands every word, but has no idea what she's talking about.

"My friend, you should get a tattoo." She unzips the top of her coveralls, revealing the multi-colored arcs of interwoven vines rising above the low neckline of the black sweater she wears underneath. She then outlines them with her finger. "I'm sure you've seen these before."

He has, though he has never before been invited to look directly at them. "I guess what I'm saying—and maybe it's not my business to say it—is that there is nothing, absolutely nothing in your outward appearance—how you dress, how you move, how you speak—to give the slightest impression that you know who you are."

He looks away, and once again moves his eyes slowly along the wire leading from the vacuum cleaner to the extension cord and into the darkness.

"And if you don't know who you are, you can't know what life is about. And if you don't know what life is about, you can't possibly enjoy it. I like you, as I said, and I want you to enjoy your life."

He is still looking away.

"You don't want to look at me?" she asks.

He turns back, looks briefly into her eyes, then lowers his gaze to her tattoos.

"A coiled snake, a sailing ship, a skull and crossbones, a bathing beauty, the word 'Mom,' whatever. If you get one you'll be taking one small idea of who you are, or could be, in this weird short life and sort of repeating it aloud to everyone who sees it. All right, maybe for you it's not a tattoo. Maybe a hat with a feather, or a mood ring, or a hotshit attitude you wear in the expression on your face." She pauses for a moment then says, "Tell me, do you trust your sexual fantasies?"

And here, he raises his arm, palm forward, to stop her from saying more.

"I know I talk too much," Victoria says, "but remember, I'm still your supervisor, at least till we punch out in the morning, so I'm going to pull rank. Just listen. Besides, listening to me sure beats the hell out of working. Am I right?"

Victoria leans toward him, with a look of concern on her face. Then she says, "Sexual fantasies are probably the truest, most prophetic dreams a person can have. In them we are the children we once were, and the adults we've become at the same time. Because of that they tell us things we should listen to. Anyone can see, just by looking at you, that once you've shot your wad into a sock or a piece of tissue, you forget the stories you jerked off to the tune of until the next time you need their help. These days, around here, acknowledging our fantasies in the daylight, even only to ourselves, seems almost impossible. In fact, that's the reason I'm leaving this town. Myself, I'm a universal donor—I love both women and men. That's why I need to live in a place where people can love whoever they choose, and where I can tell my stories out loud when I want to. Shouldn't that be an inalienable right?"

He has no answer. He can't even look at her.

Though he rarely holds the notion in mind, this man, who had been a president, has always yearned to feel the presence of someone else inside him, someone who sees what he sees, thinks his thoughts along with him, and feels what he feels. And as Victoria says these things he can't prevent himself from experiencing an odd and unexpected sensation, a feeling that she has actually been there, inside him, but he can't recall when.

"Who knows," she says, and touches his arm. "Maybe someday you'll leave, too."

"Why are you telling me this?" he asks her, quietly. It's the first thing he has said to her since she approached him and asked him to turn off the vacuum cleaner.

"Because at the moment, my friend, you're running the risk of being rudely surprised by whoever else you might be, like poor Dr. Jekyll. Or worse, of never finding out who you truly are."

Victoria falls silent and slowly rises to her feet. When she looks back at him there are tears in her eyes.

"Once I decided to leave"—she snaps her fingers—"it was just like that."

He stands up, as well.

Victoria extends her hand to him and he shakes it. "This is the only life I have ever known," she says, "and I feel like I've already left it."

Then, suddenly, her face brightens again. "Oh, there's one bit of good news—the only good news in all of it. I told the folks in the office that you were, by far, the most qualified person to replace me, and guess what?"

The man who had been a president knows he's not expected to answer, so he doesn't speak, but as it dawns on him that the two dollars more an hour a supervisor gets would mean an extra eighty bucks a week, he can't prevent a smile from stretching across his face as he nods in anticipation of what Victoria will say next.

The Wilderness of History

March 26–30

... the Now, *the unceasing chain of moments bearing the fluid substance of experience, has been growing harder to speak of and, thus, to understand. I believe this is due to the invasion of the language we speak by the language spoken to us, an idiom in which the use of the present, among the three cardinal tenses, is diminishing: More and more often, words can speak of what will happen, charged with the implication of actual foreknowledge, or of what has already occurred, wrapped tightly in a shroud of fixed meaning, yet they possess less and less the authority with which to speak for today. I fear that if the past and the future complete their advance across the territory of the present—a region occupied by nearly six billion living souls—it might no longer be possible to distinguish one from the other.*
—Emma Saint-Réal, 1986

"We want them to quit. We want them not to fight," says Harlan Ullman, one of the authors of the Shock and Awe concept which relies on large numbers of precision guided weapons. "So that you have this simultaneous effect, rather like the nuclear weapons at Hiroshima, not taking days or weeks but in minutes."
—CBS Evening News, 1/24/2003

... *the innermost principle of every war ... to aim for as wholesale an annihilation of the enemy with his dwellings, his history, and his natural environment as can possibly be achieved.*
—W.G. Sebald, *On the Natural History of Destruction*

15

Three children, ranging in age from about eight to fourteen, simultaneously get up from their seats at a kitchen table, disappear, then quickly reappear, wearing student backpacks, in a line in front of their mother, who hands them each a lunch bag before they rush out the door, run along a short paved walkway bisecting a lawn, and into the open doors of a school bus waiting at the curb. Their mother, now alone in the kitchen, looks at their three barely eaten breakfasts, shakes her head, and smiles.

He has just awoken on the couch, facing the TV, which has already been turned on with the sound muted.

Hettie, in pajamas, walks in followed by Joan, already dressed for her teaching day, squinting at a thermometer she's holding in her hand.

He sits up. The screen now fills with a press conference already in progress in the familiar briefing room in Kuwait. Hettie climbs onto the couch beside him and fixes her attention on the TV.

"I think she caught my cold," Joan says, still looking at the thermometer. "One hundred point six. She's staying home today."

He lightly presses his palm against the warm, clammy skin of Hettie's forehead.

"I'll call Ayo," Joan says. "Maybe she can come earlier."

Hettie, who likes Ayo and who is happy to stay home from nursery school, smiles, though her eyes remain fixed to the screen.

When Tom was a child his grandparents, born in the late nineteenth century, would frequently talk back to the TV. Maintaining their engagement required that they periodically interrogate this radio that showed pictures, demanding that it prove to them that it actually existed. For Hettie on the other hand—and to a large extent, for himself as well—slipping out of the embrace of the world and into the stream of sounds and images requires a transition barely more radical than lifting her eyes from a picture book and directing her gaze through a window she has looked through countless times before. Thus, to observe for the first time a man in uniform pointing a stick at a television screen that she is *seeing* on a television screen, beneath the flashing clusters of hearing-impaired captions, finds a place in her apprehension of the moment as easily as watching a scene from *Shrek*.

Tom senses that the attitude of the reporters listening to the spokesman—many of them occupying the same seats as the last time he saw them—has changed. In the first days of the war they attended what they saw and heard with the engaged, anticipatory focus of a paid audience in an infomercial, whereas now they affect the attitude of a jury withholding any indication of their response until they have carefully considered the evidence being presented. Perhaps this is because this news conference is itself a response to reports that bombs and missiles have struck residential neighborhoods more frequently than previously stated, causing a rising toll of civilian deaths.

The spokesman—in the flashed captions—is reasserting that their intelligence is good, but that Saddam Hussein's forces have been moving civilians into areas where there are known strategic military facilities, so that they can be used as human shields.

The monitor he stands before now shows a series of targets being honed in on and struck, one after the other. The footage of the two joined structures Tom saw last week is one of them. In today's versions, however, the black and white film narrations don't end on impact. Within a superimposed rectangle the non-intersecting crosshairs disappear; after the flash and milky smoke of detonation the rectangle expands and the focus changes so the audience can see—time must have elapsed—the undamaged buildings that remain standing in close proximity to the empty space the erased target had occupied, and the streets and trees below.

He speaks aloud to the TV, as did his grandparents. Hettie watches him, smiling curiously, as he tells the reporters to ask the press spokesman why, in all that footage, in the story we were watching *them* watch, there was not a single human being.

16

Tom's walking from the elevators to his office when he sees Ayo, Hettie's babysitter, along with Clara and Nalanda—all three are students in his undergraduate poetry workshop—sitting together on the window sill at the opposite end of the hall. Ayo waves when she sees him approach, then Nalanda and Clara wave as well, so he walks past the door of his office to greet them.

"What do you know," he says. "It's Moe, Larry, and Curly."

Nalanda, sitting on his right, perhaps assuming he'd named them left to right like a photo caption, lifts a handful of her long, straight, dark hair from her shoulder, points to it, and says, "You call this curly?"

"Moe, Larry, and Curly were a comedy troupe. The Three Stooges."

He's usually not in on Thursday morning—his graduate short story workshop is in the evening, and his office hours start at three—but even though Hettie didn't have a fever this morning they decided to keep her home another day. When he left she and Joan, who doesn't teach today, were playing a version of hide-and-seek in which Hettie is always the hider, while Joan, the seeker, must loudly announce each location she has looked in, without success, until Hettie shouts that it's time to be found. The game takes up the entire apartment, so he attached the file of the work he was doing to an email message, sent it to himself, and then left for his office where he can download it on to the computer and continue working on it.

"Wasn't Groucho one of them?" Clara asks.

"He was somebody else," Ayo says.

"And the funny one who doesn't talk?"

"I know him," Nalanda says. "*He's* the one with curly hair."

He hasn't completed a book in the last four years, a fact he had attributed, at first, to the arrival of Hettie in his life. He told people that rather than do anything else, even write, he preferred to spend his time in a rocking chair with his daughter on his lap, staring out the window and smelling her hair. Although there is some truth to this, he has never stopped writing in his notebooks almost daily. During those years, however, no larger form capable of containing the things he was thinking and writing has emerged. For him that has always been where a book begins. A shape, a vague outline will begin to present itself; barely visible lines will stretch between two or three of his notebook entries like the first stars of a constellation that will eventually take the shape of a measured idea. What his notebooks of the last four years document, for him, is that none of the things he has encountered in the world around him, or in his own mind, have held still or remained what they were when he first observed them long enough for him to perceive their relationship to each other.

In the last two days he has come to believe that his notebook entries since his last book appeared, including those he'd written in the days following the discovery that Joan was pregnant, in 1999, combined with the entries from this month, now nearly over, have within them the component parts of a book. He doesn't have a clear idea of how all the parts will fit together, or what the completed assemblage will look like, but he feels almost certain that for these notes from two periods of time, one incorporated within the other, the single month within the body of years, there will come to exist a container that can give a recognizable shape to the liquid substance of his words: like the woman milking a cow in Chagall's *I and the Village*, placed entirely within the huge head of another cow yet belonging there the way a heart belongs in a chest. Beyond that, the entries would not be coaxed into specific forms—the editing process would involve realizing each one so it could best deliver the impressionistic burst that caused it to be written in the first place.

❈

The more he thought about it, the more he assembled and reassembled the entries into different combinations, the more they circled around him like juggling balls, the more excited he became.

He had worried that many of the entries, if he did not create a context for them in a poem or story, would seem too fragmented, too only-his to survive the atmosphere outside the circumstances in which he had first observed them. But for Tom it is a belief he holds on to that when language is charged with the most familiar aspects of experience, with their mysterious unique actuality and the sensation of observing them, and then released into the arena of public discourse, it can attach itself to words shot like bullets in a war of continual proving and disproving, and can slow their single-minded trajectory to a rate at which we can trace their paths from source to target.

Though the brief entries in Chekhov's notebooks may not possess the complexity and articulate grace of his stories, the simple fact that Tom can sense the possibilities residing in them, more than a century after they were first written, tells him that everyone else can, as well. He wants to write a book made solely of possibilities, a book of phrases and sentences that, with the help of readers, expand until they reach places he could never imagine.

The phone in his office rings. It rings three times and stops: either one of the department administrators in the outer office, or his voice mail, has answered it for him.

He types into the computer an entry he wrote Sunday morning when he and Joan and Hettie had breakfast in a coffee shop on Avenue A:

A woman in her late forties walks up to a booth in a restaurant and waits, smiling, as the elderly woman seated there finishes lifting a spoonful of soup to her mouth, then says, Hello. The older woman, who does not speak, seems angry with the effort of trying to recognize her.

Think a minute, the younger woman says. Who comes by your apartment every two weeks?

Still no response, and then, after a moment of silence she asks, Who does your feet?

The older woman smiles now, and giggles. The younger woman leans close to her, takes her face between her hands, kisses her cheek with a loud smack.

The phone rings again, three times, and again he doesn't answer it.

Then one he wrote yesterday:

Before telling a new episode of his story, the military spokesman firmly established its shape—a rectangle—and told us that everything that happened, everything that bore meaning, would be found inside it.

There is a knock on the door, and before he can respond, the phone rings again. Then the door opens and Ayo, standing in the hall just outside, holding her cell phone to her ear and pointing to the phone on his desk, says, "You're not answering?"

He picks up the phone and she says hello.

"You've been trying to call from right here, in the hall?"

"Uh huh."

"Is everything okay?"

"Everything's fine."

He hangs up the phone then motions for her to come in.

"I don't need to," she says. "I just want to ask you something." She closes her phone, which has a charm hanging from it that looks like a bride and groom hanging on a thin chain.

She sees him notice it and steps in to show him. The husband, holding a black hat in his hands, and the bride, holding a bouquet smaller than a pencil eraser, are skeletons.

"*Calaveras?*" she says. "You know, from the Day of the Dead? They're good luck, actually."

"What did you want to ask?"

"If Hettie can come with us to the anti-war rally at City Hall tomorrow. I mean after I pick her up from nursery school, of course. This one's going to be real peaceful and boring. Nuns and old hippies and students. Everyone holding candles and stuff."

116

"Who's us?"

"Nalanda and Clara and me."

"I don't know. In the last week demonstrations have gotten a lot more serious. So have the police. I'll talk to Joan about it."

"Joan already says it's okay with her. As long as Hettie goes all day today without having a fever. Did you know my friend Cleo's in Joan's class? She said Joan's the coolest teacher."

"She is."

"Yeah? I told her *you* were the coolest teacher."

A male voice behind her says to someone in the hall, "He's in there?"

Before the speaker receives an answer Tom sees Nick, his graduate student and author of "The Plumber's Divorce," standing in the open doorway.

"Hey," Nick says.

"Can we talk again later?" Tom asks Ayo. "I want to think about it a little more."

Nick moves aside to let her leave, but remains standing just outside the office. "Since you're here early today," he says, "can I take you to lunch?"

17

"You sure you don't want this?" Nick asks, pointing with his fork at the uneaten enchilada on the plate Tom is holding over Nick's side of the table.

"I'm sure."

Nick rakes the enchilada onto his own plate, along with the remains of a puddle of red sauce. While eating Tom's leftover enchilada as quickly as he ate the two that came with his own order, he points his fork at the front half of a yellow 1950s-era Studebaker, sitting in the center of the large dining room, about five feet from their table. It has a lit taxi sign on its hood, a Mexican license plate on the front bumper, and the name of the restaurant on its side door. "You think that was once a real car that somebody drove?" he asks.

"Sure," Tom says. "It's still real. The way dinosaur skeletons in the museum are real."

"It's like a car that was real until somebody put it in a story."

Tom laughs. "A story so short they could only fit half of it in."

Nick appears to think about this for a moment, then says, "I want to thank you for all the reading you've done for me this semester. I know you don't read as many stories by other students."

"None of them write as many as you do."

"How about coffee? You want some coffee?"

"I'd love some."

"I know the revision of 'The Plumber's Divorce' has all the stuff that was missing in the last version," Nick says, continuing the discussion they had yesterday in conference. "I mean, now it has the things it sort of implied it had, but didn't. And it has them in ways that make it the reader's story, too."

"That's a good way of putting it."

As the waitress clears the table Nick orders coffee and a fried ice cream, then looks to Tom, who just asks for coffee.

"But getting back to the story," Nick says, "even with all that added stuff, I like the first version better."

"How so?"

"I like it best when writing a story is sort of like being told a story. Not that I mind the work. I don't. But I prefer to be the one who's listening, the one waiting to see what will happen next. After I finished the revision, I reread that first draft, and I had the feeling of excitement I had when I first wrote it. Sure, it wasn't as strong this time, but I still felt it. When I read the second version, it wasn't there."

The waitress approaches with two mugs of coffee in one hand and, in the other, a stainless-steel dessert dish with a sphere of fried ice cream the size of a baseball.

"You think that's because I wrote stories for so many years without ever showing them to anybody?"

"I think it's as simple as the fact that you only want to write stories that are good."

The waitress sets the two mugs in the center of the table, and the fried ice cream in front of Nick. She takes a dessert spoon and two new napkins from the pocket of her small apron, and then, from the same pocket, she takes out her check pad and a pen. "Anything else?" she asks.

"If it's not too much trouble." Tom says and points to Nick's ice cream, "I think I'll have one, too."

Nick smiles, pleased that he has influenced Tom's decision to also have dessert. Then, suddenly, something on the other side of the room takes hold of his attention.

Tom turns and tries to see what it is, but the fender of the Studebaker blocks his view. "What?" he asks.

Nick leans off the side of his chair, squints, stretches his torso and neck to get a few inches closer to whatever it is that he sees, then says, "*No.*"

"No?"

"For a minute I thought I saw someone I knew." He falls silent, but appears to grow more agitated. "It couldn't be her," he says. "Besides, she said that if she *was* coming, she'd call first."

He leans off the side of his chair again, then stands and looks across the room. "It can't be," he says and drops back into his seat. "Fuck, shit, piss, it *can't* be her."

"Who?"

"Sadie."

"Sadie?"

"My wife. My ex-wife."

"She's here?"

"It's not like we're enemies. We still email each other, and sometimes talk on the phone."

"She's here?"

"She said she might be coming to New York in the spring. She just finished her master's—she's a speech therapist—and she might be interviewing for a job in a clinic somewhere in Brooklyn." He gets up, steps over to the Studebaker, looks toward her over the roof, holding his hand above his eyes to better focus his stare under the fluorescent lights. Then he comes back to the table.

"It's her," he says. "But why didn't she call? She said she'd call if she was coming. And what the hell is she doing in Manhattan?"

"You sure it's her?"

He gets up, looks once more, quickly, then sits, takes a spoonful of ice cream and with dramatic nonchalance brings it to his mouth, as if doing so would make his weird behavior seem less conspicuous. "I'm sure. I think she even looked back at me, but from this distance she'd never be able to see me without her glasses."

The waitress comes by and sets the second fried ice cream on the table, along with the check.

"Wait," Nick says to her. "Can we get one more of these?"

She points at Nick's fried ice cream, at the single small crater left by the spoonful he's just eaten. "Something wrong with that one?"

"It's not for me." He points toward the table where the woman he's been looking at is seated. "It's for her."

"Who?"

Nick stands, leads her to the near side of the yellow Studebaker, and points over the roof toward the woman seated alone.

He returns to his seat, shivers, and says to him. "I'm sure now. It's her." The waitress returns to the table. "You know her?" she asks Nick.

"I do."

"I don't want to get in the middle of something weird."

"He does know her," Tom tells the waitress, and holds out his fried ice cream to her. "Bring her this one. Then you won't even have to change the check."

"But that's yours," Nick says.

"I ordered impulsively. I was moved by how you spoke of your writing and somehow, at that moment, it made me want dessert."

"He's my professor," Nick says to the waitress.

Tom's still holding the ice cream. "Take it," he says to her.

Nick, becoming even more agitated, watches the waitress walk off with the dessert, but then looks down at his hands, clasped in front of him on the table. "Can you see?" he asks.

Tom gets up, walks around the other side of the Studebaker and then watches the waitress approach a table beside a window near the front where a woman with dark hair is seated alone, reading a paperback. He first tries to see in this young woman's face and posture some aspect of the plumber in Nick's story, but realizes that if the character were to look like anyone in the real world, it would be Nick. He returns to the table.

"Did you see her?"

"I saw the waitress arrive at her table. That's all."

"You think I should go over to her?"

The waitress walks past them without looking up on her way back to the kitchen.

"You think I should go over there?" Nick asks again. "Or should I wait another minute?"

"I think now's the time." Tom starts to get up.

"You're leaving?" Nick says.

"I have to get back. Besides, you guys aren't going to want me around."

"Wait," Nick says, rising to his feet. "Please just wait till I get back." He then quickly walks off.

Tom takes his notebook out of his pocket, sits down again, but finds he doesn't have a pen, which, though he had nothing in mind to write, causes a wave of panic. He flips through the pages, but doesn't read anything. Then he slips it back into his pocket.

A moment later Nick is standing across from him, his hands on the back of his chair. "I can't believe it," he says. He walks around to the front of the chair and sits. He leans forward, props his elbows on the table, and drops his face into his hands. "It's not her." He covers his eyes.

"What did she say?"

"Up close, she doesn't look a thing like her. What is my fucking problem?"

Tom sees the young woman approaching, carrying the dessert dish with the fried ice cream. He reaches across the table, clasps Nick's forearm, and nods toward her just before she reaches them.

Nick straightens up.

"I usually don't eat dessert with lunch," she tells Nick. "If I just left it sitting there it would go to waste."

"Do you eat dessert with supper?" Nick asks her.

"Sometimes," she says and smiles, then sets the ice cream in the center of the table.

"I'm sorry," Nick says to her. "From this distance . . . "—he points toward the table where she'd been sitting—"you look so much like someone I know. This is my writing professor. He doesn't eat dessert with lunch either."

"How do you do?" she says to him, and shakes his hand. "I'm Lily."

"In fact," Nick says, "He hardly eats a thing till supper."

"This is Nick," Tom says to Lily. "One of the best new writers on the island of Manhattan."

"Wow," Lily says. "There must be a lot of writers in Manhattan."

"He writes fiction, among other things," Nick says to her. "You can't expect him to tell the truth."

"I'm hardly exaggerating," Tom says. He then reaches over and slides back one of the two empty chairs at the table. "Would you care to join us?"

She sits. "Who did you think I was?" she asks Nick.

Nick can't answer. He looks at Tom.

"Would you like some coffee?" Tom asks her. He looks around the room for the waitress. "I'd like some more."

"I don't drink coffee," she says. "I drink tea, though."

He catches the waitress' eye and motions for her to come.

"Now everybody's here," she says when she arrives.

"This woman would like some tea," Tom says.

"Herbal," Lily says. "But not the kind that will make me sleepy."

"Red Zinger?"

Lily nods.

He holds up his coffee mug.

"A refill?" she says, then turns to Nick, who's looking down at the tabletop, his face soaked with tears.

After a moment of silence he looks up at the waitress, then at Tom, then at Lily. "I'm sorry," he says.

Lily looks back at him, surprised, thoughtful, curious. "For what?" she says.

18

Back in his office, he clicks into his email then opens the first of the two messages that Jimi sent him the night before last.

It was great talking to your wife this evening. It was nice of her to let me chew her ear off for a while. Please thank her for me. And also, please tell her that Laurie and I have decided to put off the move—at least for a year or so. We're going to think about it for a while.

But who knows what the future holds? Anything can happen, like our running into each other after so many years!!!

Let's try to keep in touch.

Your homeboy,

Jimi

He opens the second email, the one Jimi was probably writing while Tom was sitting on the couch, trying to take his pulse by the VCR's digital clock.

You deserve a better explanation. Or, with apologies in advance, I need to give you one.

The nice thing about email is that you don't have to disturb anybody, especially late at night, and you don't have to hear somebody's response to what you say right after you say it.

As he reads he hears, for the first time, the voice of the adult Jimi has become.

Anyway, here's the story. Last summer Laurie and I decided to spend a few weeks on the Maryland shore. When the kids were younger we rented a house there every summer. She and the kids would stay all week, I'd come out for weekends. We hadn't gone since Andi left for college. That same year Michael hit full adolescence and the last thing he wanted to do was spend that much time away from his friends. It was nice, being there, just the two of us, a kind of warm-up exercise for the empty nest. In fact, that's when we first talked about selling our house and moving to New York.

It rained most of our second week there, and the climax, two days before we went home, was a night of thunder and lightning out of the Old Testament. Somewhere nearby a power line got struck and sent an electrical surge through half the houses on the beach front. It blew out the screen of the TV that Laurie happened to be watching at the time, and fried the motherboard in my laptop, even though I had a surge protector.

As we were driving back to DC Laurie said, What if it wasn't the storm, and I said, What if what wasn't the storm? And she said, You know, the power surge. So I said, Now you've really lost me.

Let me ask you a question, she said. What if a bunch of terrorists became electricians—it's got to be easier than becoming pilots—then got jobs with the power company and waited for their chance to cause a power surge that could paralyze half the country?

I reminded her that this was just a few houses on the beach. And that there happened to be a very serious electrical storm.

But what if they timed it that way? she asked. Because this one was just practice. Sort of like the first time they bombed the World Trade Center. So I told her, you know what, Laurie? You got a terrific imagination. It sounds like a great plot for a novel. Then I told her about you—I swear. I didn't know that like six, seven months later I'd run into you. I said there's this guy I knew in high school. He became a writer. Maybe we can get in touch.

Anyhow, three nights ago, she had a dream that terrorists detonated an atomic bomb in the Atlantic Ocean just a few miles off the coast of New York. She woke terrified. I asked her why she thought they'd do that and she said because that's exactly what no one would expect them to do. First a tidal wave would flood the whole city. Then a nuclear cloud would blow radioactivity all over everything. Her fear only got worse the next day. She began talking about her dream as if it was a prophecy.

I kept telling her it would never happen. It sounded more like a disaster film and nothing that happens in disaster films ever actually happens. I said it's ten times more likely that you and I would win the goddamn lottery for once. And she kept saying, how do you know it will never happen?

We had dinner after I spoke to your wife today. Laurie seemed *calmer and didn't mention bombs the whole time. I told her I was glad to see that she was feeling better, and she said thank you. Then she said, There's still one thing. What about the power surge they made last summer? The power surge they made? I repeated, but then I didn't say another word because it finally got through my thick skull how utterly frightened and how transformed by her fear she truly was.*

All the years we've been married she's never worked. Her whole life has been the kids. Now all the shitty, scary business in the world has gotten mixed up with the kids growing up and moving out of the house.

There was more: an apology for going on so long, and another request to keep in touch.

He still has twenty minutes before the first conference. After that he has an open office hour, then workshop at six-twenty.

The phone rings again, three times, and stops.

Tom closes the email and the work that had been on the screen before reappears, a few lines he wrote in his notebook on Monday morning, the day after he encountered Jimi for the first time in more than thirty years.

He reads them now as if Jimi were reading along with him.

Who wants to walk home every day past
that same guy bending down, picking up
a cigarette butt, bringing it to his mouth,
or, for that matter, that bum always asleep
on a park bench? Soot-darkened bricks
are frames in a too-sad black and white
movie we should no longer have to bear.

Edit out the missing front tooth, the toe poking
through a hole in a gray sock, the two children
staring at a dead cat in an ash can. Easy
as changing a channel, easy as a magic word—
presto—they'll no longer line the tangled maze
of streets beneath the jazz skyline, the path
leading all that way, all that way, to here.

Before he even finishes, the lack of interest he imagines in Jimi's response becomes his own.

He takes Emma Saint-Réal's *Collected Essays* from the shelf and reads a passage from her unfinished essay, "Our Presence," written shortly before her death in 1990. He then types it out, and as he watches the words appear on the screen of his computer, he imagines Jimi is reading them as well:

We make music that can link the inner lives of strangers. We construct beautiful bridges that defy gravity, and powerful swift trains that give as much pleasure to watch passing as to travel inside of. We have long since determined, via science and poetry, the existence of more dimensions than our senses tell us we occupy.

We have produced a device that can do the work of failed kidneys; we can forecast weather, cultivate sweet plums, observe the behavior of the component parts of atoms; we can draw blood from one body without doing it harm and infuse it into another, giving it life.

We adopt children and know them as our own, and send words and pictures to the edge of the universe. We can heal, nurture, and thrill with touch, use science and technology to make ourselves beautiful just for other people to see, and can be made happier by the sight of warm sunlight falling through a window onto the worn boards of an old wooden floor than by the things we do and own.

He has finished his conferences and is halfway through his open hour. So far, no students have shown up.

The phone rings. This time he answers it.

"It's Nick. You got a minute?" He hears a rush of traffic and voices and a siren, which he also hears from the window.

"Are you right outside?"

"You must be psychic."

"You're not going to believe the last few hours I've had," Nick says, sitting in the chair that faces his desk.

"Tell me everything. Or at least as much as you can tell me before workshop starts. That's twenty minutes."

"We stayed in the restaurant a while. She sipped her tea and I ate the second fried ice cream that no one else seemed to want. Then we went to the park. I told her about being married, about almost becoming a veterinarian. While I was talking to her I realized that just before Sadie and I split, when I discovered that I wanted a different life, too, it didn't mean I didn't love her. But I think, for her, a different life also meant she didn't love me. At the time I kind of vagued out on that part. The truth of it is that she left me."

"You told all this to Lily?"

"No. I just told her the other part. About how much I had wanted a life totally different from the life I was living at the time I was married to the person I mistook her for in the restaurant. Then she told me about her life. She's a lawyer, do you believe it? But she doesn't want to be. No more than I want to be a veterinarian. Because she graduated second in her class she got this plum job right out of law school—as a clerk for a state supreme court judge in Albany. That's where she's been living. That's where she's still living. Anyhow, she recently felt like her life had always been a dream. It wasn't one of those stories where somebody had pressured her into becoming a lawyer. But when it actually happened, when she *became* a lawyer, she had this growing feeling that there would never be another thing she could ever be. At first, she thought it was just fear. Fear of being a grown-up, fear of not having any more second chances. So she stayed with it. Spent all of last year clerking for this judge who is a nice lady, but this year, in fall, when the school year began, she discovered that what she really wanted to do was teach young children. Once she realized that, she didn't wait. She found this program called the Teacher Corps where they invite people in other professions to become teachers. She was here for her interview. It was this morning. She does two months of training this summer and begins teaching next fall. She's got to

128

leave first thing in the morning. Catch a train that will get her up to Albany by nine.

"It's the kind of coincidence that only happens in movies. I mean, the last place either of us expected to be was here. "

"Will you see her again before she leaves?"

"She's waiting for me in the park. I wanted to ask you if it was okay if I missed workshop tonight. If I give you the stories that will be talked about"—he pulls them out of his backpack—"could you give them to Quincy and Olivia? And tell them I'm sorry?"

"What a day," Tom says.

19

After making an entire orbit around the painted-steel fence that surrounds City Hall Park, preceded by the walk west from her nursery school on East Broadway and now to Vesey Street and through the gate leading into the churchyard of Saint Paul's Chapel, Hettie is ready to sit down. She climbs onto one of the benches beside the entry to the chapel. Tom sets her backpack beside her, folds up the stroller she did not ride in but walked alongside of, and sits down himself. "Know what?" he says to Hettie, who is looking at the rows of old gravestones and the people walking on the paths between them, "I think you have just completed the longest continuous walk you have ever taken." He attempts to count the series of blocks they have just walked on to approximate an idea of distance, but cannot recall enough of them to assemble an accurate estimation.

She slides off the bench and points to a headstone located halfway between them and the fence that borders the churchyard on the west, across from which is the tall fence and blue-painted plywood perimeter of Ground Zero. Eight or ten people have gathered around it. They arrange and rearrange themselves so they can take each other's pictures standing or kneeling beside it. Hettie hasn't asked about the old stone chapel nor about the weather-worn headstones, many of which have stood there since the eighteenth century, but she's curious about why these people are so interested in this one.

She walks toward them, stops halfway, turns. When she sees him begin to rise to his feet, she spins around and runs the rest of the way.

The view of the headstone itself is blocked by the people standing around it. And as he and Hettie wait for their turn to approach it, he can see that the churchyard rests on a north-south running spine of slightly elevated land that extends through this entire section of lower Manhattan like the linear bump on the crease of an unfolded map. From here the land, by small, long degrees, slopes downward, and when he looks across the filled-in marshland that includes the World Trade Center site, and through the spaces between the buildings just west of it, he can see the eastern shore of New Jersey. At the time this chapel was built and the people laid to rest here, there must have been an unobstructed view of the river, which would have been close enough for the naked eye to easily see in it the reflection of the sky.

"Sir?" someone right behind him says.

He turns and finds himself facing a woman in a security guard uniform. She has wheeled over the stroller, still folded, and holds Hettie's backpack with the straps over her wrist.

"You can't leave this there," she says.

"I'm sorry," he says. "She headed over here so fast . . . "

"It's not because anybody'd steal it, though they might, it's that you don't leave anything unattended here." She nods toward the fence surrounding Ground Zero. Nothing you want back, anyway." She then looks down at Hettie and says, "Hi, Precious."

Hettie smiles, though she's looking down at her feet.

"I've got a granddaughter about your age," she says to her, "and a grandson who's six."

Hettie turns, and surveys the churchyard, particularly the people in it.

"No. They're not here," she says to Hettie, attempting to read her thoughts, as adults do with small children, and perhaps reading them correctly. "They're at home with their mama on Roosevelt Island." She points over her own shoulder, toward the east. "That's a *real* island, right in the middle of the other river."

"She ran over here because she was curious about what made this stone so special," he tells the woman.

She slowly shakes her head, clearly annoyed. "They're always crowding around Mary," she says, "not that any of them are related."

"Nobody gave her a thought until *that*." She nods again toward Ground Zero. "For more than two hundred years she was resting in peace. Before that, all she ever did, as far as anybody knows, was get born and die. Then, suddenly, she became everybody's great-great-great-great-great grandmother."

"I don't understand," he says.

"You didn't know about her?"

He shakes his head.

Now there are only three people there, one of them focusing a small digital camera, the other two kneeling on each side of the stone.

"Come on, Precious," she says to Hettie and takes her hand. She then steps in front of the woman holding the camera, squats down in front of the stone, and shows them the words on it.

Hettie is disappointed with the stone itself—there is nothing special about it—but is happy to have gotten close to it.

In Memory of
Mary Wife of
James Miles
Died Sep 11ᵗʰ.
*1796 in the 37*ᵗʰ
Year of her Age.

※

With Hettie now in the stroller, they are walking along the paths that begin at the fountain and wind through the southern portion of City Hall Park, the only part since 9/11 that people can walk through freely. Since they left St. Paul's he's been speaking to Hettie about the things they passed, hoping that the ride in the stroller, accompanied by the sound of his voice amidst the hive of voices and traffic sounds, would help her fall asleep. He described the intricate stonework on the façade of the Woolworth Building; he read the various historical plaques with words and illustrations etched into flat stones set in the sidewalk pavement:

The British Soldiers' Barracks, 1760
The Old Firehouse, 1859–1870
The Dispensary and Soup House: located on this site 1807–1835:
Served soup to imprisoned debtors and other impoverished New
Yorkers.

Before they left the cemetery, the security guard had squatted down and showed him the inscription on another gravestone just inside the gate leading back out onto Vesey Street.

"I like this one," she said.

He squatted beside her. Hettie stood between them.

Here lies the body of
James Davis Late Smith to
The Royal Artillery Who
Departed this Life 17th Day of
December, 1700, Aged 39 Years

Behold and See as You Pass By
As You are Now so Once was I
As I am Now You Soon will Be
Prepare for Death and Follow Me

Hettie grew restless as he read it aloud. The security guard took her hand and said, "Precious, this world still holds a million surprises for you. But I don't think any of them are in here."

As they stroll, he considers what the woman said to her just fifteen minutes earlier, and adds his thoughts about those words to the procession of things he's been telling her in a voice similar in tone, though louder, to the voice he uses when reading her to sleep.

"When the world is new, it doesn't hold surprises. I've learned this from you, in the three-and-a-half years of our acquaintance. Each new thing you see is simply *there*. Like the stuff that appears the moment you turn on a light in a darkened room: That stuff isn't surprising—not because you expected any of it to be there, but because the existence of anything you come upon for the first time, you accept as a fact the moment you encounter it—and maybe that's because the growing collection of already-there stuff in your world is no less remarkable. The business of being surprised comes later."

When they reach the point where he can see the arches of the Brooklyn Bridge and the graceful web of suspension cables slung between them, he tells her about the morning that he and her mother were married. Hettie, eight months old, was present, along with the two friends who had come with them to City Hall to be their witnesses. While they were sitting nervously in the first row of folding chairs in the waiting room outside the small chamber where the Justice of the Peace would perform the wedding, the two friends who accompanied them presented Joan with a garter belt, each holding it by one side so they could read the words embroidered in black script on the pale silk: *Too Sexy to Be a Wife*. Hettie wore it as a headband in the photos they later took at a point half way across the bridge, where they walked after the ceremony.

Tom keeps talking to Hettie, even after her eyes have closed, though some of what he says now, he says only in his mind. A half hour ago, the first time they crossed the northeast corner of the park where the rally was scheduled to begin at four o'clock, there were few signs that anything out of the ordinary was expected to happen there. In the time since, two lines of police barricades have been placed in the street, creating a walkway that encircles the sidewalk at the outer edge of the pedestrian island, extending beyond the fence; that includes City Hall and the park, and police are watching green-uniformed workers setting up another barricade walkway that leads from the street to the subway entrance. Although they might find themselves close enough to shake hands, people not involved in the rally and those participating in it will be kept apart.

Close behind them a driver leans on his horn to express anger at a cabbie who has stopped in the one moving lane of downtown traffic on Park Row—the barricade-walkway has taken up the lane nearest the curb—and Hettie wakes up, or seems to, and looks around without focusing her gaze on anything. When he resumes speaking aloud she lets her head fall against the back of the stroller and closes her eyes again. Barely realizing it, because he was talking to himself, and in something like the shorthand syntax he uses when writing quickly in his notebook, he'd been telling her about something that happened during the May Day March on Washington he'd gone to, just weeks before he graduated from high school in 1970. The memory became the dream embodying his anxiety at being here with Hettie, and his increasing uncertainty as to whether they should leave now or wait a bit longer.

That same spring of wild car rides with Jimi and friends, his girlfriend had managed, through her older sister, a student at Queens College, to get seats for them on a charter bus carrying a crowd of antiwar protestors to Washington. They'd managed to get separated during the day and at one point, in early afternoon, he found himself in a crowd of older demonstrators rocking one of the National Guard busses in an attempt to turn it onto its side. It was close to falling over when they heard teargas canisters clunking onto the pavement behind them. He ran along with the others, and when he had gone maybe twenty-five yards he stopped, turned, and saw that one young man, barely older than himself, was still leaning his shoulder into the bus, which hadn't yet toppled over the other way, or rocked back onto all of its tires, or rocked back even further to fall on top of the young man; but before Tom could see what happened, the wind, coming toward him from behind the bus, blew the cloud of teargas into his face. The sting penetrated his skin, and entered his open eyes and his throat and nose, and burnt like fine, sharp acidic sand—he'd never felt anything like it before—and he turned and ran again, blindly, until endless minutes later someone led him to a plastic bucket of water, dunked a bandanna into it, and pressed it lightly to his face, which made the exposed skin burn even more. He has remembered that day, clearly, many times since. It was the moment that shoved him off a path he'd been on since childhood, a route he hadn't even known he'd taken until he changed direction. He is afraid even now for the young man, who might still be standing with his shoulder against the mammoth weight of the tilted bus.

❖

They are standing near the subway entrance between the fence surrounding the park and the edge of the sidewalk, at which point the enclosed barricade walkway, now complete, splits into a T and runs north and south in the first traffic lane on Broadway.

A police officer is standing beside him—though Tom hadn't noticed his approach—smiling down at Hettie. He is a young man, in his early or mid-twenties; the name on his nameplate is Ruggieri.

He watches Hettie for another moment, then says to Tom, "The last few months my son refuses to fall asleep in his crib, so I wheel him around in his stroller. My wife'll be asleep already, so it's just him and me—back and forth, back and forth. I talk to him, too, even after his eyes are closed, just to make sure he doesn't wake up." He removes his hat and slips a wallet-size photo from the band inside and hands it to Tom: a small boy in yellow pajamas standing in front of a Christmas tree, steadied by an adult hand reaching in from outside the frame, holding him by his shoulder. The picture must have been taken three months ago, but it could've been taken in 1950. "Almost nineteen months," he says, slips the photo back, puts on his hat, and says, "You guys headed for the subway? If not you'll have to stand outside the walkway."

Officer Ruggieri points to the barricades behind them, on the side farthest from the area where the rally will occur. Before Tom can turn he notices something sail across the upper range of sight: he looks up and sees a leaf, spiraling silently downward like a biplane with engine failure—above eye level, then at eye level, then close enough to grab, which he tries to do, but misses, and watches it land, without disturbing her, on the lap of his sleeping daughter. He bends and picks it up by the stem: a perfect maple leaf, dry as old parchment, that must have hung onto the branch it grew on and later died on, until today. He turns, now, in the direction Officer Ruggieri had been pointing to, and sees that a crowd of onlookers has gathered. He also sees Ayo, with Clara and Nalanda, slip under one of the barricades and walk toward them. When he turns back, Officer Ruggieri is nowhere in sight.

"What's that?" Nalanda asks, pointing to the leaf.

Tom holds it out to her.

Ayo and Clara both squat down. Ayo kisses Hettie's forehead and then they both pass under the barricade and weave through the crowd toward the center of the area where the rally will take place.

"I'll stay with you guys," Nalanda says. She takes the leaf from his hand, but it breaks off at the stem and she lets it fall.

Everything, suddenly, is moving faster. Circles have formed and are growing denser. A line of police officers in riot gear is surrounding the central area Clara and Ayo have walked into like the first ring around a bull's-eye. A circle of onlookers surrounds them, and a third circle, this one also of police officers, but not in riot gear, is forming around them, with their backs against the barricades he and Nalanda and Hettie are just on the other side of.

The walkway is crowded, mostly with onlookers, though people going to and from the subway manage to work their way through a narrowed channel in the middle. Behind the barricades on the other side of the walkway is a crowd made up of the first wave of people getting off work, some of whom slow down in order to see what's going on, some of whom do not. They are a shore beyond which extends the rest of the city.

"Oh," Nalanda says, "I forgot to explain why we were late. You know what we did?"

Hettie begins to stir, but doesn't wake.

Nalanda kneels down beside her, quietly strokes her arm, and whispers to him, "We went to her nursery school first. Ayo forgot we were supposed to meet here."

"I think we're going to leave." Tom looks toward the congested walking lane along Broadway. It isn't moving—everyone in it has stopped to watch, and he can't see over the backs of the police officers in front of them, so doesn't see what they're seeing. Getting to the subway entrance will be easier.

"You know, it's supposed to be real boring," Nalanda says, "Like a vigil."

"I'm not sure why I brought her here in the first place."

"Hettie and I are friends," Nalanda says. "I hang out with Ayo a lot when she babysits." Hettie seems to be peacefully asleep. "You guys have the coolest apartment."

He leans against the barricade, looks through the space between two officers. He can see a dense circle of people, at least thirty feet in diameter, most of them sitting down. He sees among them an elderly couple he remembers from the Union Square rally, other people in business suits. There are a number of the "old hippies" Ayo had spoken of, but most of the people in the circle are the age of his students. Three or four of them, standing near the middle, are spinning slowly to display the placards they are wearing, front and back, that proclaim "The World Says No to War": English on one side, Arabic on the other.

"Since Ayo knew you were going to be here, she decided to go into the circle. I'm the one who'll stay here with Hettie in case you want to go in, too. Kind of like the designated driver."

"We're going to leave," he says again.

The people in the center circle, the bull's-eye, have begun to chant, *No war for oil, No war for oil, No war for oil.* Soon, a growing number of voices from the eddying circles of people around them join in, as well.

He sees Clara, sitting near the placards in the center, looking back in his direction, stone-faced, not seeing him. He cannot see Ayo. The chant is now coming from the people behind him and from those crowded into the walkway on Broadway, too.

Three figures with their heads and torsos inside large papier-mâché masks of Rumsfeld, Cheney, and Bush wade through the crowd behind him, playfully waddling and squeezing between people, working their way toward Broadway.

The chanting grows louder, and when he turns he sees that the people immediately behind the last barricade are animated and chanting, too. Despite the deafening mantra, Hettie has not stirred in her sleep. The skin of a child's sleep can be sheer and porous, or leathery and tough; it's impossible to know how this flock of voices might enter her dream.

In spite of the growing size of the crowds, and the knowledge that people were protesting all over the world, the atmosphere at the rallies he'd been to during the weeks and months leading up to the war were characterized by a tentative curiosity, a fear of believing that what they opposed was truly real, and the uncertainty that a gathering of individual bodies, even when numbering in the hundreds of thousands, could ever again stand against the forward advance of a history that does not appear in its terrible actuality, but as an immense forest of words.

This war is now an ongoing fact and the chant reverberating in expanding concentric circles isn't so much a shout aimed at the deaf ears of leaders, but a swelling evocation of the need to first comprehend and then express to ourselves what it feels like to live inside this moment. Perhaps because they sense something more unified and thus more threatening in this, or perhaps because they have been sent a signal no one else is aware of, the police in riot gear begin to close in on the epicenter. As they do so, the wider circle of officers, whose backs are directly in front of him, spread out to allow the people standing around to pass between their bodies and squeeze under the barricades.

Tom should leave now, and will, but wants to see Ayo first.

Once the crowd of those standing has thinned out he sees that she is no longer sitting beside Clara, who still appears stone-faced and unfocused, but nearer the opposite side of the circle, not facing outward but almost toward them, shivering with fear.

He turns to find that Nalanda is now holding Hettie in her arms. He folds up the stroller, but before he can pull the strap over his shoulder, Nalanda takes that, too. Hettie sighs a breath-long cry of complaint and presses herself closely to Nalanda's chest, but does not wake.

Police with plastic handcuffs are now moving among the protesters, who are all sitting or lying down. One at a time they bind their hands behind their backs and hoist them to their feet. Still, many of those within the circle do not appear to realize that everything in the moment, without a word spoken loudly enough to be heard, has changed. Two officers walk directly to the center and take the placards from those holding them as if they were potential weapons.

They are quickly bringing to an end a demonstration that has not even truly begun; acting as if this group of non-violent protesters has grown into a dangerous and unpredictable mob.

A few of the people in the walkway with him slip under the barricades and move toward the circle, in order to join those being arrested.

The area must have been charted beforehand, decisions made as to where the wooden barriers should be placed, where the police would form lines with their bodies. The organization of space became the organization of time: this carefully determined division of less than an acre of urban space was the prediction of a future they are now, with military efficiency, causing to bring about.

Only a few people remain between the barricades and the people being arrested. Clara is now standing with a group of twenty or twenty-five people who've already been handcuffed. Fewer and fewer demonstrators are entering the now shapeless circle. Even so, there are enough of them to slow the process by which the police officers are working their way, person by person, to the edge of the circle where Ayo is sitting with her head resting on her arms, crossed on top of her drawn-up knees.

Nalanda loudly calls to her. She raises her head, and when she sees them her entire face is suddenly overtaken by the act of crying, as a young child cries, the skin clenching tightly around the eyes, her mouth tearing itself open wider and wider.

She had placed herself in this situation to make a statement, yet she could not have anticipated what it would feel like. In that way, this twenty-year-old who cares for his daughter like an older sister is also a child. Like so many young people he has known, she possesses a humane regard for the world, yet has lived most of her life quarantined from history, and thus, from a part of herself as well.

Ruggieri and the other officers in regular uniform have joined those in riot gear, making even larger the extent to which they outnumber the demonstrators. No more than a dozen people are still waiting to be arrested.

Since most of the police officers are as young or barely older than the students they're now arresting, they must regard them with the instinctive sense of familiarity shared by members of the same generation, yet they approach each of them as if they might suddenly slip out of their civilian cocoon and spread their terrorist wings to reveal the belt of explosives hidden underneath.

"Do you have a cell phone?" Nalanda asks him.

He shakes his head.

She hands him Hettie who, amazingly, is still asleep, and feels even heavier. He is frightened. He unfolds the edge of her cotton cap so that it covers her ears as well.

Nalanda then pulls out her phone, pokes in some numbers, and holds it to her ear. "Damn," she says. "I'm trying to call Ayo but she's not hearing her phone or doesn't want to." She leaves a message: "We're still right here, Ayo. Ayo, we're looking at you."

Ruggieri and another officer, a woman, are now pulling Ayo to her feet.

He hands Hettie back to Nalanda, then squats and passes under the barricade and walks up to Ayo, whose hands are now bound.

"Hey," he says.

She looks at him but says nothing. He imagines that if he

touched her face her skin would feel warm, as if she has a fever.

"Stand away," the woman officer says.

His arm is pulled and bent behind his back. He is then yanked away from Ayo. He feels a hand take his other arm and another grab him by the shoulder and spin him around.

The woman officer faces him now. It is she who has spun him. The hands holding his arms behind him slide down to his wrists and try to pull them together, but he pulls one of them free. The hand behind him then grips the wrist again and this time the policewoman pulls out her nightstick and holds the top of it under his chin.

He nods toward Ayo, "What has that girl done?"

"I don't want to use this," the policewoman says.

"My daughter is there." He nods toward the barricades. "She's three years old. I will not let you hold me."

She shoves her nightstick through the loop on her belt, turns him away from her, adds her grip to the other fixed to his wrist, yanks it down hard. This time he pulls the other hand free.

Ruggieri is now standing there, facing him.

Two other officers are holding his arms, but his hands have not yet been brought together. He's furious and he's frightened and when he speaks he's not sure if it sounds like he's crying. "My daughter is there," he says, directly to Ruggieri, nodding again, and then ripping one arm free.

The two officers behind him move again to restrain him but Ruggieri raises his hand.

Tom points to the automatic in Ruggieri's holster. "I won't let you stop me," he says, knowing how stupidly dramatic he's being, and knowing, as well, that there's nothing else he can say.

A cell phone rings.

"That's mine," Ayo says.

"It's Nalanda," Tom tells her. "She's right there."

"All of Joan's numbers are in the contact list in my cell." Ayo , now thinking clearly, says.

"Let me give that phone to the girl with my daughter," he says.

"Then you can arrest me if you want to."

"You're an idiot," Ruggieri says, angrily. "You're an idiot for bringing her here in the first place."

"Where's your phone?" Ruggieri asks Ayo.

"In my pocket," she says. "I give you permission to remove it."

"We don't need your permission," he says.

The woman officer withdraws the phone from Ayo's pocket, opens and closes it, then hands it to Tom.

The other two officers lift their hands from his shoulders.

Ruggieri, furious and entirely impersonal now, says, "Okay." The woman officer walks ahead of him, Ruggieri stays just behind as they begin to cross the short distance to where Nalanda is standing, holding Hettie.

With each step, the world gathered around them steadily flickers: it is itself, a mosaic of pixels, itself again. . . .

The distance between Tom and the female officer has grown. Ruggieri puts a hand to his back, pushes him to walk faster.

There seems to be a program, a barely discernable choreography guiding the movements of everyone here, now, six thousand miles from this horrific war but, from inside the experience, the dance has no meaning beyond its insistence on continuing.

Yet from the other side of the barricade, or from a passing car, the events of this moment might appear to be what we expect such a moment to appear to be, the way we know, when observed from a distance, what a soccer game is, or a picnic. And later, when seen framed in the soft-edged rectangle of a TV screen, narrators' voices worming through its liquid colors, we will know exactly what it is, because it will conform to the shape of what we already knew it to be.

Tom has just contributed a small portion of meaning -- he could do nothing else: An unarmed man, older than the officers restraining him, makes a small gesture of resistance and, in not masking his fear, has offered himself to their moral authority. They've seen things like this in movies, heard of them in stories read to them in elementary school classrooms. Tom has given them this: something familiar, identifiable, a single part of the experience they can stretch across its entirety, so that when they rebroadcast it in memory, they can leave out everything else.

They do not stop him from reaching below the striped plank of the barricade and helping Nalanda open the stroller. She lays Hettie in it. "She's going to wake any minute," Tom says to her. And then, to Ruggieri, he says, "I'd appreciate it if you'd escort her to the subway entrance. And I'd be grateful if you'd help her get the stroller down the stairs."

"I'll be okay," Nalanda says.

Hettie opens her eyes—perhaps she sees him—and then closes them again.

Nalanda flips open her cell phone, pokes something, and Ayo's phone, which he is still holding, begins to ring.

"Sorry," she says. "I didn't mean to hit redial."

Ayo's phone rings once more, then stops, before he hands it to her.

Ruggieri is looking at the two calaveras, the bride and groom, swinging back and forth on the chain. "What are they, skeletons?" he asks, though the question isn't addressed to anyone in particular.

"All of Joan's numbers are in here," Tom tells Nalanda. "Home, office, and cell. If she doesn't answer, leave messages. Tell her you're bringing Hettie home." He reaches into his pocket. Before he can withdraw it the woman officer seizes his wrist.

"My keys," he says.

She loosens her grip, takes the keys from his hand and gives them to Nalanda.

He turns to Officer Ruggieri. "You were right before."

"About those charms? They're skeletons?"

"You were right that I was an idiot for bringing my daughter here."

20

Tom wakes before the phone's first ring completes itself and, during the quiet syllable before the second ring, he hears the theme from *Sesame Street* snaking through the louder, circumambient drumming of the shower: since he was still sleeping, Joan left the bathroom door open so she could hear Hettie if she were to call her.

It rings again, then a third time, and his sense of the moment condenses to the singular awareness that if the fourth ring starts, the answering machine will kick on in the kitchen at the other end of the apartment and he won't be able to hear the voice of the caller leaving a message, should that person choose to do so.

He lifts the handset off the phone beside the bed.

"Hello."

"Is Joan at home?" a woman's voice.

"Who's calling?"

"I spoke with her yesterday."

Could it be Jimi's wife, too shy to introduce herself? Had she called Joan after all?

"Can she call you back?"

"She doesn't have to bother. If you can tell me when she'll be there, I'll call again."

This is not Jimi's wife. There's something too officious in her impersonal, calm-voiced refusal to actually answer a question. A solicitation? Worse. Something to do with his being arrested yesterday? The FBI? He says nothing more.

Hettie, having heard his voice, walks in, stands beside the bed, and watches him holding the phone. She's wearing one of his T-shirts, a green one that fits her like a choir robe.

"Is there a good time to call back?"

"Who are you?"

Hettie sharpens her focus on his face.

"Joan and I spoke yesterday."

"Can you hold one moment?" He sets down the phone, lifts up

Hettie, and swings her onto the bed beside him. He then picks up the phone and says, without raising his voice, "It's now today. And you're talking to her husband. So just tell me who the fuck you are."

"I'll just try at a more convenient time. Thank you."

***

He's sitting on the couch with Hettie watching *Dora the Explorer*.

Joan walks in drying her hair with a towel, stands beside the couch and watches with them.

He tells her about the phone call from the woman who said she'd spoken to her yesterday, but Joan doesn't respond. Dora and her sidekick, a monkey called Boots, have just fallen into a hole, and Joan's watching as intently as Hettie. In a circle that fills the top half of the screen are five of the things Dora carries in her backpack: a pair of scissors, a map, a roll of tape, a book, and a coiled length of rope.

The voice of a narrator, in English mixed with Spanish, asks which of the things will help them get out of the hole.

"Which one?" Joan asks Hettie, who keeps her eyes on the screen and says nothing.

After a quick beat of silence, a chorus of children's voices says, "The rope," then, "*la cuerda*," and suddenly one end of it is in Dora's hands and the other end is tied to a tree growing close to the edge of the hole.

"For a second I thought it might have been Jimi's wife. But then she got weird and official like maybe she was the cops, wanting to arrest me again. Who'd you talk to yesterday?"

"It wasn't the cops," she says, but before she can say more, the phone rings again. She walks into the kitchen, returns a moment later, and hands him the receiver. "It's a student. Nick, I think."

"Lily just called and told me you got arrested," Nick says. "At an anti-war rally? At City Hall?"

"How did she know? There wasn't a word on the news last night.

I haven't yet read the papers this morning. Does she know . . . wait." He picks up a sheet of paper he'd left on the table and reads from it. "Charlotte Engel? She's a lawyer from the ACLU. She called me last night after I got home."

"I don't think so. She called to offer *her* services, in case you needed a lawyer."

"So how does she know?"

"She heard it on the radio early this morning. A public radio station she gets up there in Albany. She said forty-eight people had been arrested. But they only mentioned two names. You and some other guy, Jonas Somebody, a retired physics professor from Columbia."

"None of us were booked or charged with anything. Officially, we were only detained."

"I'm not sure what that means."

"Ayo and Clara were arrested, too. After they got us all in plastic handcuffs, they arranged us in a line against a fence. While we were waiting, Jonas Asrelsky, who could have been eighty years old, nodded toward this statue next to a fat tree on the other side of the fence right behind us, and shouted to the cops, 'We've got a reporter embedded with us,' and this young cop named Ruggieri comes up to him and asks what he's talking about, and he says, 'See what it says on the pedestal? I'll read it to you: *Horace Greeley, Founder of the New York Tribune*. He's writing down every word you say.'"

"Wow," Nick says. "That almost sounds like fun."

"It wasn't fun. While we were waiting they decided to search us again. Just to pass the time. Then two school busses pulled up. They loaded half of us into one, and half in the other. We had to get in the back, because everything behind the driver was really a cage. The next stop was another cage at the precinct house. That one was large enough for everybody. From the moment they locked us up not a single member of the New York Police Department had a thing to say to us. We were on our own. Then, nearly three hours later, they released us without a word of explanation.

"For a few hours we were dangerous criminals. Then we went

home. I walked in the door at exactly nine o'clock. I could have sat on the couch and watched Larry King if I'd wanted to."

"What are you going to do?"

"The ACLU lawyer said there would be a class-action suit, but she didn't say what that would entail." He hears a call-waiting beep, and sees Hannie's name and number on the caller ID. "Oh shit," he says.

"What?" Nick says.

Another beep.

"Oh shit," he says again. "Nick, there's another call. I have to take this one."

"Don't worry," Hannie says, after he hits the flash button and says hello. "She's okay."

"Good." Tom exhales, then says, "And you?"

"Every chance I get, I'm up there with her watching movies. It's like the two of us are taking a bath in movies."

"Wow," he says.

"I'm calling about something else. Victoria. You made quite an impression on her, you handsome devil."

"I did?"

"I ran into her yesterday, crown of thornless thorns and all, and we had a nice talk about you. I mentioned to her that you were a writer and right away she said she had to get in touch with you. I told her I'd call you, before giving her your number."

"Did she tell you why she wanted to call me?"

"She wants you to write something about her brother."

"I'm not sure if I can," he says. "But I'll certainly talk to her

"Good," Hannie says. "Gotta go. I'm heading up to the Bronx. Today's matinee is a double feature: *After the Thin Man* and *Shop Around the Corner.*"

Last night, when Charlotte Engel called, the first thing she wanted to know was if the officer who'd arrested him had warned him that he was breaking the law.

"He called me an idiot," he told her.

"Did he say anything else?"

"Not much."

She explained what she thought the police had intended to do. The plan had been to wait until the demonstrators stayed beyond the time limit of the public assembly permit, and then arrest everyone still in the area designated for the rally. "That's a tactic they've used a lot lately. Unfortunately for them, their watches were running fast. Also, before arresting anyone, the police are first required to ask that you leave the area, and then inform you that if you don't you're breaking the law. They seem to have forgotten that part, too, and that part, not following proper protocol, is worse than jumping the gun."

❊

Tom is pouring a second mug of coffee when Joan walks into the kitchen with Hettie who is dressed except for her shoes and coat. On Saturdays Joan often brings her to a play date with the five mothers she met four years ago, in prenatal yoga, and their children—Nellie, Marina, Ai, Amanda, and one boy, Jacob—all of whom were born within weeks of each other.

Joan sits on the floor and begins to slip Hettie's shoes onto her feet.

"Who called earlier?" Tom asks her.

"Nick?"

"Before Nick."

"Oh, yeah, I forgot. Remember that woman who stayed here once? . . . In the old days before you knew me?"

"Who?"

"The one who wasn't your girlfriend or anything but who you slept with every night for a month?"

"Not every night."

"Apparently, she had acquired a lot of student loans, none of which she paid back. So yesterday, while you were on your way to the slammer, a collection agency called. Actually, a guy called first. I told him that he had the wrong number, and he read the number back to me and it was right, so I told him that he had the right number but the wrong person. Five minutes later a woman called. Probably the one you talked to. Maybe they have better luck with gender-coordinated calls. By the time I realized they were looking for Nibor, your lost love, and why, I might have given her the impression that I had some knowledge of who she was. At that point Nalanda called. I saw Ayo's number flash on the Caller ID screen so I just cut the lady off."

She stands up now and looks at him angrily.

"The first thing she said was, 'Hettie's with me. I'm on my way to your place. She's fine.' It was like she stopped before finishing a sentence that ended, 'but *he's* dead.'"

Joan begins to weep, yet maintains the same angry-ironic composure.

He stands up, but she motions for him to sit down again.

"Then it occurred to me," she says, "that a good thing to ask would have been 'Where's Ayo?' since Nalanda was calling on Ayo's phone and not saying anything about her, either."

"She told you we were fine?"

"Of course she told me you were fine."

❖

A half hour after Joan and Hettie leave, the phone rings again. A man asks for Thomas.

"Who's calling," Tom asks.

"I'm calling regarding . . ." and after a pause, "a misunderstanding . . . "

"Who's calling?" Tom asks, sharply.

"Earlier, you might have had a misunderstanding when an employee of our agency called."

"And you are?"

"Her supervisor."

"You want to know about Nibor Whelan, am I right?"

The man, surprised by his taking a direct path to her name, takes a moment to recover. "Evelyn?"

"Why didn't you just say that up front?"

"I apologize."

"She was my girlfriend. A long, long time ago. That's why my wife didn't know anything about her."

"I see."

"Have you spoken with the family?" Tom asks.

"*Her* family? I haven't been able to make contact with them."

"I know they miss her very much."

"They do?"

"Of course they do. She was so young."

"Has something happened to her?"

"You don't know?"

Tom receives no answer to this.

"I don't know how else to say it, except to tell it to you straight. She died."

"When?"

"On 9/11."

"We never got word."

"Wait. You never got word and you haven't contacted the family? Does that mean you think Evelyn Nibor Whelan was her real name?"

"It's not?"

"It was her name for a while, but never her real name. You don't know anything about her, do you?"

Again, no answer.

"Look, I don't know who you are, or if you even have the right to know, but I'll tell you. Mary—that was her real first name—and Miles, that was the last name she went by since shortly after we broke up and she met her future husband James. She'd had a drinking problem for many years before I met her, and in that time she'd done a lot of things she preferred not to remember. So part of what helped her get a new start in life was a new name. That make sense?"

"I guess . . ." He pauses, then asks, "You're telling me, then, that Mary is her real first name and that, for the last several years she's used the last name Miles?"

"I'm telling you that. Soon after that terrible day they laid her to rest in the cemetery of St. Paul's Chapel in lower Manhattan, in sight of Ground Zero. If you're still looking for her, that's where you'll find her. The stone carries her real name."

"Please forgive my having to ask this, but is that Miles with an 'i' or Miles with a 'y'?"

"Look for her with it spelled the first way you said it, with an 'i'. You might find that you're not the only one visiting her grave. There are many who miss her."

21

He had planned to spend all of Friday morning and early afternoon—before he picked up Hettie at nursery school and walked west to City Hall Park—revising the opening of his book, but instead he pulled books off the shelves in their apartment, one after another, read a page of Charlotte Brontë, three lines by Paul Celan, paragraphs from James Baldwin and W.G. Sebald, and bits and pieces from the works of other writers who, if they were alive today, would be far more likely than he to find words, and forms in which to contain them, that would throw some comprehensible light on this historical moment.

As a student, Tom had read an essay by Heinrich von Kleist about the act of thinking while speaking to someone else. Kleist advises the reader that if you find yourself struggling with something you cannot understand, but urgently wish to, you should enter a conversation with an acquaintance. This need not be someone with any special knowledge, nor should you ask for help in solving the mystery; you just say what it is. Then, as you speak, you discover, hidden within the constellation of your own thoughts and memories, the inkling of a solution already in your possession: like a brief phrase in one of Chekhov's notebooks in which reside the basic molecules, the as yet unspoken words that will tell an entire story.

What Kleist is proposing is that within the process of conversation—even if it is largely an inside job, like the dialogue Tom's grandparents carried on with their television, or the agreement festivals we participate in with our other selves while drinking alone—those words will gradually realize themselves and, like the image in a slowly developing Polaroid, the solution to the problem will likely emerge. Often, without being aware they are doing so, he and Joan have helped each other in this way.

On Friday morning, in reading from the works of these different writers, Tom was asking for the same kind of help. After a time, he began to copy some of the excerpts he'd read into his notebook. Reading what they had written was like going back in time and drinking the clear water that had once flowed in a now polluted stream; copying out their words offered sustenance and pleasure— like playing a Beethoven piano sonata from sheet music instead of listening to a recorded version.

Even so, the help he was seeking did not come. There never had been a golden age, and the context within which these writers labored to produce their works—even the most recent of them— were very different and thus, in each case, provided a different historical music to the words. This moment—the context Tom writes in—is the month containing the first days of an unprovoked war, inexplicably abetted by much of his nation's mass media: a war not fueled by the defense of its borders, or a long-felt enmity, or even by Olympian rage, but rather a war viewed as a calculated means to ends beyond conquest—likely among them the theft of its own democracy—waged with an unprecedented wealth of weapons and an idiot's witless disregard for the actuality of other human lives.

❖

"Tom," Hettie says, when they are halfway across Broadway. She is pointing at a man sitting on the sidewalk, leaning against the wall of a bank on the corner they're approaching, wearing an unbuttoned green flak jacket with no shirt underneath, holding a Starbucks cup out in front of him. The man keeps his eyes forcibly closed the way a child does during a scary scene in a movie. He does not open them as they approach, nor when Tom drops the change from his pocket into his cup.

There are fewer cars parked on the street. As the weather grows warmer, more and more people leave town for the weekend, and the day feels unusually quiet.

"Maybe we should go away for a few days," he says to Hettie.

"Go away?" she asks, and points ahead of them. She just wants to continue along the path toward home.

Walking east along the quiet streets, holding his gaze just above street level, today could be any Sunday in the past seventy-five years. Nothing within his line of sight speaks of the world at a distance, or of the benumbing chatter and flash flickering on the screens of TVs.

Tom thinks of the moment when Ayo slipped beneath the police barricade and walked into that frightening circle: She was not simply protesting the unprovoked invasion of another country by her own country. She was—though she may not have understood it in these terms—participating in an act of resistance against a voice that's been whispering this persuasive offer to an entire population, one person at a time: Stay on *that* side of the barricade—from there, if you want to, you can view the horrific evidence, without having to know yourself as a citizen of a nation at war. You can, in other words, bear witness without being changed by the thing you behold.

He worked on the book again this morning, before Joan left for her office and he and Hettie went to the park. He found that arranging the various entries continues to be the easiest, most pleasing part. He likes their different shapes, diverse subjects, how some are better than others, and how they are unequally possessed of meaning. However they combine and recombine, they always, in the words of Muriel Rukeyser, one of his favorite poets of the last century, "touch like islands underneath." For him that is the pleasure of working on the book, placing himself within the space occupied by the small clusters of words, repositioning himself in that space each time he juggles them into a new constellation. Finishing, in a sense, involves fixing them in place, and enlarging that space to include the world outside the book, and this he realizes he cannot do on his own.

The book he's writing should not begin with written words. It should begin with black and white footage from a nose-cone camera of a precision missile approaching its target, or with someone's story told over a cell phone, or with a TV commercial, or with Puck addressing an audience from the outermost edge of a stage. It is a book that cannot be written by him alone. The changing historical circumstances, the pages the individual columns of words will be printed on—and the readers themselves—will also have more to say. In the nearest future he will write something else, perhaps a book about Victoria's younger brother, or someone like him.

※

Hettie stops in front of the Daughters of Bethlehem home to watch two men trying to lift one of the two large front doors off its hinges. One squats, his shoulder against it, his arms reaching as far around it as they can—still not completing a full embrace—while the other, standing awkwardly over him, holding the edge with only his hands, tries unsuccessfully to maintain a firm enough grip against its enormous weight. They stop, step back, look at it, and try again with no more success than the first time. Then one of them goes inside and the other lights a cigarette.

Tom looks through the clean windows, at the bright white walls of the empty rooms. "Do you think it's haunted?" the sales agent had asked him. In a an earlier century, perhaps in a future one as well, her surprising and youthful beauty, clothed in the uniform of a business suit and the older-person role she was enacting, might have presented a provocative contrast similar to that of the fur-covered china of Meret Oppenheim's cup and saucer. But in this time and place such radical juxtapositions have lost their startling mystery, and for language to overcome this condition it must give way to the world, it must disappear in the process of conveying each impression it briefly captures.

The man who'd gone inside is now back out front, slipping the flat end of a long pry bar under the door. Then, squatting and pressing down on the bar while the other stands with his torso against the door's edge, they manage to lift it off its hinges, set it on the ground, and lean it back against the other door. Then, both standing, they lean it forward, lift it again, carry it a few steps toward the sidewalk where Tom and Hettie are standing, and lay it across two saw horses. Without saying a word, the men step close to each other, face them, remove their hardhats and give a bow. Hettie giggles. The younger of the men, probably eighteen or nineteen, walks up to her, kneels, removes one glove, holds his hand up, palm forward, and without hesitation she gives him a high-five. The two men then walk back inside.

Tom tries to steer them toward home but after a few steps the younger man walks back outside dragging a long orange extension cord. He smiles at Hettie, who will not take another step, and dramatically loops the wire around the doorknob as if he were performing a trick with a lariat. When he's done he extends the wire to the end of the table nearest to where they are standing, and drops it with the plug dangling over the end. He tips his hardhat again to Hettie and this time sets it on the door. He removes his gloves, and sets them beside it, removes an iPod from the pocket of his thick flannel shirt, adjusts it, runs a pair of earbuds up to his ears, and slips it back into his pocket. He puts his gloves back on, though not his hardhat, and walks back into the building.

The young man returns with a large belt sander, which he plugs into the extension cord. He turns it on, off, on again, and begins to move it along the edge of the door in a slow, steady rhythm, one that might match the rhythm of the music only he can hear.

"Tom," his daughter says, and points to the young man, though she knows he is already watching, as well.

Tom turns, looks at her, then follows her stare back to the young man, who now seems lost in a private dream, a story he is telling himself to the rhythm of his work, and perhaps she called Tom's name because she sensed what he is sensing now, that she and her father, this girl of three, this man of fifty, standing less than ten feet away, could be involved in this young man's dream.

"He will someday have a daughter," he says to Hettie, whose gaze is lost in the wide-swaying ribbon of sawdust falling like flour beneath the sander, carpeting the sidewalk and collecting on the tops of the young man's work boots. "Just like I do."

They will remain there a moment longer, and in that time Tom thinks of the entries he will write in his notebook when he next gets the chance:

"A police officer doesn't yet know that he will later arrest the man to whom he is showing a photograph of his young son."

"An old man pointing to a statue beside an old tree: *It's an embedded reporter!*

"A homeless man, pressing his eyes tightly shut, holds out a cup."

"A young man sanding the edge of a door dreams he has

a daughter. As the sander moves back and forth she grows to adulthood; as the sander moves back and forth he realizes that in this moment, late in the morning of March 30th, 2003, he is, at the same time, performing a familiar workday task, and doing what she—his daughter, this citizen of a wholly unimaginable future—will see him doing when she imagines the life he lived in the years before she was a part of it."

Notes

The brief phrases from Chekhov that appear in this novel are from *Notebooks of Anton Chekhov*, translated by S. S. Koteliansky and Leonard Woolf. B. W. Huebsch, Inc., New York, 1921.

The essay by Heinrich von Kleist referred to on page 151 is "On the Gradual Formulation of Thoughts While Speaking," a fine translation of which (under that title) appears in *Selected Prose of Heinrich Von Kleist*, translated by Peter Wortsman. Archipelago Books, New York, 2010.

The phrase quoted from poet Muriel Rukeyser on page 153 is from her poem "Islands", *The Collected Poems of Muriel Rukeyser*. McGraw-Hill Book Company, New York, 1978.

Thanks to Brian Breger, Breyten Breytenbach, and Jocelyn Lieu, who read earlier versions of this book; and thanks to Hanging Loose editor Dick Lourie, whose thorough, engaged work on the manuscript helped me see this novel more clearly. Thanks to Robin Tewes for bringing her artist's eye to the words. Thanks to Marie Carter for her skill and patience; to Steve Gibson for the seed of a story within the story; to Christopher Baughman who lent a dozen of his good words; and to my new colleague, Harold Davis.

Commonplace book: *A book in which one records passages or matters to be especially remembered or referred to with or without arrangement.*
The Oxford English Dictionary